Going Solo

Howard Martin

Going Solo

ISBN-13: 9798686178359

Going Solo

This is a work of fiction.
Names, characters, businesses,
places, events, locales, and
incidents are either the
products of the author's
imagination or used in a
fictitious manner. Any
resemblance to actual persons,
living or dead, or actual
events is purely coincidental.

Cover image by Fidelity Design
and Print, Unit 7, Kenneth
Way, Wilstead Industrial Park,
Bedford, MK45 3PD, UK,
www.fidelityprint.co.uk
quotes@fidelityprint.co.uk
Tel: +44 (0)1234 907907

CHAPTER ONE

Roger and Alison were eating breakfast.

'So, where did you get to last night, Alison?' asked Roger. 'You certainly weren't at work until 11:30.'

'Oh, so you are taking an interest in me now, are you?' replied Alison. 'That makes a change. Maybe I got taken on a trip to Le Touquet or something.'

'Now you are being silly.'

'And where were you, Roger? With your Floozie, I expect.'

'I was at the club. I had a flying lesson, then I went into the bar and met some friends.'

'Friends, or one particular friend?'

'Well, Mandy was at the club. She sometimes works behind the bar.'

'Yes, but she wasn't working last night, was she?'

'How could you possibly know that?' said Roger. 'Unless of course, somebody told you. Someone who knows her quite well. Dan the Eunuch, perhaps?'

For once, Alison had no answer. She sat silent for a moment before deciding to go on the offensive.

'OK Roger, I admit it. I was with Dan. Now, will you admit you were with Mandy?'

It was Roger's turn to be silent. If he admitted he had been at the club with Mandy, what would Alison's next question be?

He decided to come clean. 'Yes, I saw Mandy at the club. But we were both a part of a larger group.'

'Did you ensure her underwear was on correctly before you parted? I'm sure Dan would have checked when she got home.'

Roger said nothing.

'You do realise Dan is thinking of starting divorce proceedings against Mandy, as I am against you if you don't stay away from her.'

'But I can't help but bump into her when

I go for my flying lessons, she works behind the reception desk!'

'Simple answer Roger, give up the flying lessons. I still need the money for the granny flat.'

'Oh, right. Threaten me with divorce to coerce me to give up the flying lessons so you can use the money to bring the wicked witch to live here. No, never.'

'Oh, you are impossible, Roger. Stay away from her, you have been warned. I'm going to work.'

Alison got up and slammed the door behind her. BANG!

No, I'm not giving up flying thought Roger *Life is beginning to be interesting and fun.*

CHAPTER TWO

Roger walked into Flight Training reception.

Mandy was behind the counter.

'Hello Mandy, how are tricks?'

'Not good, Roger, not good at all.'

'What's the matter?'

'Dan got very nasty last night, insisted on checking my underwear.'

'So, is he a bit of a pervert, as well as a Eunuch?'

'No, to be fair I think he was just checking I hadn't got them on backwards and inside out again. Luckily, I hadn't.'

'You know he was with my wife Alison, last night?'

'No, I didn't. He never said. But it confirms what we suspected. How can you be sure?'

'Well, Alison was trying so hard to be clever, she let it slip. She also said both she and Dan are considering divorce as an option.'

Mandy fell silent for a moment. 'Oh, this is getting serious, isn't it Roger?'

'Well, you would have to ask Dan. I wouldn't trust Alison to be telling the truth. She can be as slippery as an eel when she's trying to get her own way. She's already tried blackmail this morning.'

'What do you mean?'

'Well, she said divorce was an option if I didn't stop seeing you. When I pointed out you worked where I was having flying lessons, she said I should give up the flying lessons, as she still wanted the money to build the granny flat.'

'What did you say?'

'I told her no way. Life has just started to be interesting and enjoyable for me.'

'Well, tonight I must ask Dan what he is really thinking.'

'Do you know what happened at the club last night? Did the police arrest many?'

'Yes, I heard from Forsythe this morning it was six. Apparently, the police phoned

Jed first, as they didn't realise he had sold the club.'

'Oh, he must have been delighted!'

'Indeed, so Jed gave them Forsythe's number, and he came in. He sacked Chantelle on the spot, poor girl.'

'Well, it wasn't her fault. She was brave enough to try to break it up.'

'Yes well, that's Forsythe for you. He said it needs men to run a bar and keep people in order, and he had the ideal pair in mind.'

'What, two blokes you mean?'

'Yes, that was what he said, so we perhaps we can look forward to Clint Eastwood and Arnold Schwarzenegger running the Linton Flying Club bar.'

'I'm not keen on Clint Eastwood myself. He lost me my first job.'

'What? Clint Eastwood did?'

'Well, indirectly. When I was a teenager, I used to change the advertising on the front of the Zonita cinema in town. Unfortunately, when I put the letters of his name up, I accidentally put the L and the I in CLINT far too close together. And with the cinema being right next door to the Strict Baptist chapel, the manager got dozens of complaints. He wouldn't accept it was a genuine mistake, and he fired me.'

'Oh no!'

'All water under the bridge now. Anyway, I've got a lesson booked, and I'll be going to the bar afterwards. Can you join me?'

'Yes, but not for long. I don't want to upset Dan.'

The door to Lewis Davidson's office opened and Lewis appeared with Jane. He kissed Jane on the lips. 'See you later, darling.'

'Can't wait,' she replied as she walked to the door.

He turned to Roger. 'Hello Roger, the weather is a bit rough this afternoon, so how about sitting the Air Law exam? If you don't pass, you can always sit it again. But you must pass that exam before I can send you solo.'

'Yes, OK Lewis. I think I have a good knowledge of Air law.'

'Well come into my office, and we'll do that. Mandy, we are not to be disturbed.'

'OK, Lewis.'

CHAPTER THREE

Roger walked into the bar with a spring in his step. Passing the Air Law exam had given him a boost. Another step towards his lifelong ambition.

'Can I help you, sir?' The deep voice boomed around the empty club.

Roger looked behind the bar and saw a strange man standing there. He was about 5ft 6in tall, slightly foreign-looking, with his hair greased back to reveal a high forehead, and a big nose with a small moustache beneath. He had quite a muscular frame, spoilt only by a beer belly overhanging his belt.

'I'll have a pint of bitter, please,' said Roger, 'I've not seen you here before.'

'No, we've only taken over today,' he

boomed, 'I am Kingsley and my partner is Fidel.'

'Did I hear my name taken in vain?' A shorter man emerged from the cellar. He had wavy hair, was clean-shaven and wearing dungarees. His voice was in complete contrast to Kingsley's, being considerably higher pitched.

'Ah Fidel,' said Kingsley, 'meet our first customer.' He turned to Roger, 'And you are?'

'I'm Roger. Roger Moore.'

'Delighted I'm sure,' said Fidel, 'I've always wanted to roger more.'

'Now behave yourself, Fidel. Pleased to meet you, Roger. Here, this pint is on the house.'

'Oh thanks, Kingsley,' Roger raised his glass, 'Your very good health, err to both of you. And more to the point, good luck with running this bar!'

'Why do you say that?' asked Kingsley, 'We were told it almost ran itself. Just crews, pilots and the like.'

'Well, that may have been how it was when Jed had the bar, but since Forsythe has taken over he has opened it up to everyone. Six men were arrested for fighting last night.'

'Oh, the bastard,' said Fidel, 'he never mentioned anything about that before we signed the contract.'

'You signed a contract to run this place?' asked Roger incredulously, 'How long for?'

'Two years.'

'Good luck with that! You may need to employ bouncers or perhaps reduce the membership back to the flying community.'

'I don't think we can reduce the membership. I think the contract said we would actively work to widen the membership to all.'

'OK, back to the bouncer option then!'

'Well we shall have to play it by ear, but with the range of beers we shall be offering and the delicious home-cooked food, I hope to attract a better class of clientele.'

'Yes,' said Fidel, 'it's going to be a nice place for nice people.'

CHAPTER FOUR

'Hello, Roger.'

Roger turned and found Guy had crept up behind him.

'Bit quiet today, isn't it?' said Guy, 'I guess the police arrested all the customers last night.'

Behind the bar, Kingsley winced. 'I sincerely hope not!'

'Ah Guy,' said Roger, 'this is Kingsley and Fidel. They've taken the bar over as of today. Kingsley, Fidel, this is Guy. He provides entertainment in the club.'

'Pleased to meet you, Guy.'

'Pleased to meet you too. Kingsley, Fiddle.'

'It's Fidel, not Fiddle, thank you, Guy,' said Fidel with a scowl, and walked off to serve another customer.

'So Kingsley, what did the contract say about entertainment?' asked Roger.

'I think it said we had to provide good entertainment for the customers.'

'Sorry Guy,' said Roger, 'looks like you are out of a job.'

'Ha, bloody ha, Roger. Kingsley, I do a disco every night plus a grab-a-granny dance on Sunday. Would you like me to continue?'

'Err, yes please, Guy. As Roger said, we only took over today, and we have so much to organise in the way of beer and home-cooked food, entertainment is the very last thing on our minds.'

'Sounds like you've got something in common there then Guy!' said Roger.

'Oh you are on form today, Roger,' replied Guy, 'Did Mandy give you a really good seeing to last night or something?'

'Or something, actually. I've just passed my Air Law exam.'

'Oh good. If only I knew what that was, I'm sure I'd be as pleased as--.'

'The pint is in, I tell you.' a man shouted, 'I haven't been here for two months but I'm sure Jed will confirm it if you ask him!'

'I'm sorry, sir,' said Fidel, 'but we only took over the bar today so all outstanding transactions have nothing to do with us! Four pounds, please.'

'I tell you the pint is paid for. Can't you check with Jed?'

'I've never seen Jed, but I'm told he sold the bar to Forsythe. Take it up with them. Now the pint is four pounds please, or I shall have to ask you to leave!'

The man turned purple but sensing Fidel's mood, put his hand in his pocket and put four pounds on the bar.

'Who the hell is that,' asked Roger.

'Oh that's Bomber,' replied Guy, 'He flies for Sleazy Jet. His real name is Peter Jones, but he's better known as Pompous Pilot owing to his unreasonableness. Never argue with him. He'll bring the argument down to his level, then beat you with his experience.'

'Yes, he does sound a bit Bomberbastic.'

'Oh, there's no stopping you today, is there. You've even invented a new word. Passing Air law has really cheered you up!'

CHAPTER FIVE

'So you've passed Air Law, Roger? Well done!'

Roger turned and George stood there smiling. 'Thanks, George.'

'Do you know who owns the N registered Lear Jet that's parked outside the club?'

'I've not seen it. What do you mean by N registered?'

'N registered means it's from the USA. It's unusual for one to be parked at the club.'

'It wasn't there earlier. Mandy might know. We can ask her, as she said she would pop in for a quick one before she went home.'

'Did she mean a drink or something else?' enquired Guy.

'Well, you can ask her that question

yourself Guy, if you dare. Here she comes now.'

'Hello all,' said Mandy.

'Hello Mandy, can I get you a drink?'

'Yes please, but only an orange juice, I can't go home smelling of alcohol.'

'OK, one orange juice and a pint for you George? Now Mandy, while I get the drinks, George has something to ask you.'

Roger lent over the bar. 'Fidel, can I have an orange juice and a pint of bitter please.'

'Yes Mandy. What is that N reg Lear Jet doing at the club?'

'Oh, right. It belongs to a rather brash American called Dick Dangler. He didn't like the fee the airport wanted to charge him for parking on the apron, he wanted something cheaper. So Air Traffic sent him over to the club. After some argument, Lewis agreed on a charge for parking outside the club.'

'Dick Dangler?' said Guy, trying not to laugh, 'that can't be his real name. It sounds the sort of name Sid James would have in a Carry-On film.'

'Well he will probably be in here soon,' said Mandy, 'He's gone to book a room in the airport hotel, but he said he likes a drink, so I told him about the club bar.'

'Well one of us must go to the gents with him when he goes,' said Guy, 'See if he lives up to his name!'

Roger smiled to himself. 'Mandy, I don't suppose he has left a key to the aircraft with the club?'

'Down boy,' replied Mandy, 'I must go home soon, Roger. No time for fun tonight.'

'Howdy folks.'

Everybody looked round. A man in a white suit and a white Stetson hat had walked into the club.

'How do. I am Dick Dangler from Chattanooga, Tennessee, and I'm very pleased to meet y'all.'

He looked around at the startled faces. His eyes rested on Mandy, the only person that he knew.

He glided across the floor, elbowed Roger out of the way and put his arm around Mandy's shoulder.

'Mandy, my dear. You are so pretty. So this is the club you were telling me about.'

'Yes Dick, this is the Linton Flying Club bar.'

'Well it's pretty too, you know. Rather small, not like our bars in America but cute

18

all the same. So who owns it? These guys behind the bar?'

'It's owned by a man called Forsythe, but I'm afraid I've never met these two before.'

'Let me introduce you then,' said Roger, removing Dick's arm from Mandy's shoulder, 'this is Kingsley and Fidel. They've just taken the bar over today.'

'Well, I'm right pleased to meet you folks, Kingsley and Fiddle. Let me buy all you good folks here a drink.'

Fidel scowled 'It's Fidel actually, Dick.'

Dick replaced his arm around Mandy's shoulder. 'OK bartender, please get all these good people whatever they want to drink, and yourselves of course.'

Guy pulled Roger to one side. 'Dick seems to have taken a real liking to Mandy. You better keep an eye on her. Her knicker elastic is a bit suspect at the best of times. One yank and they'll be off!'

CHAPTER SIX

Captain Slack and his crew came into the bar. Sandy spotted Roger and came over. 'Hello Roger, you can buy me a drink now if you like.'

'Hello Sandy, what would you like?'

'I'll have a G and T please.'

'Here let me buy it,' said Dick putting his free arm around Sandy. 'Bartender, a G and T over here, please. This place is so full of pretty ladies. I see you are in uniform, my dear. Which airline are you a hostess for?'

'I fly for Sleazy Jet and I'm a pilot, a first officer to be precise.'

'Oh dear, I don't think women should be pilots at all,' remarked Dick, 'it's a man's job.'

Sandy unhooked his arm, turned and

faced him. 'Why? What do you think a man can do that I can't?'

'Nothing, but you ladies have periods and go mad for at least one week in four. I sure as hell wouldn't want you flying me around when the curse descends upon you!'

'You male chauvinist pig.'

'Are you alright, Sandy?' Captain Slack turned and sprang to her defence.

'Oh, this yank thinks I shouldn't be a pilot because I have periods. He wants me in the cabin serving drinks.'

'Oh, does he now?' Captain Slack rounded on Dick. 'And who the hell are you?'

'I'm Dick Dangler from Chattanooga, Tennessee, sir. It's my Lear Jet parked outside the club.'

'Well Mr Dangler, I suggest you fly it back to Chattanooga and your toothless friends, probably to the sound of duelling banjos. We may not be politically correct with our humour over here, but let me tell you we don't tolerate sexism or racism in practice. For your information, I am a training Captain for Sleazy Jet and I can tell you, Sandy is an excellent pilot all four weeks of the month.'

'Well sir, you are as entitled to your opinion as I am to mine. But I come from a God-fearing country, where the women-folk are primarily there to look after the men-folk.'

'Really? I thought you had slaves for that. Plus some original design ideas for bed sheets and pillowcases!'

Dick was shocked. 'I've never been a member of the Ku Klux Klan.'

'Oh, perhaps your bloodline wasn't pure enough. Maybe your parents weren't brother and sister. I hear it's a popular relationship in the Deep South.'

'Now lookee here Mister,' said Dick, letting go of Mandy and putting his face close to Captain Slack's face, 'You are starting to grate on my nerves.'

'Good' said Captain Slack with a smile 'then I think you've finally got the idea none of us like downright rudeness. So if you'll apologise to Sandy, we'll say no more about it.'

Everyone in the bar started to laugh. Dick was shocked. He looked around at the laughing faces and realised he was the fool.

'I'm waiting,' said Sandy.

'Oh um, I'm sorry, my dear. I didn't

mean to upset you,' said Dick, 'but you have to realise different folks have different ideas and culture.'

'Apology accepted,' said Sandy 'and I realise but, do you? The fact we Brits think of the deep south of the USA as a hotbed of incest, religion and racism seemed to upset you.'

'Well at least in the USA we call our inbreds hillbillies. In England, I think you call them the Royals. Oh hell, look at the time, I need to take a leak and return to the hotel for dinner. Where can I find the gents?'

'I'll show you,' said Guy and Roger together, 'I'm just going myself. This way.'

Sandy turned to Captain Slack. 'Thanks for supporting me, James.'

'No problem, I meant every word of it.'

'I didn't realise you were so politically correct.'

'I'm not politically correct, Sandy. I hate it. Free speech is so important. That man has a perfect right to his views, dreadful though we think they are. Mr Dangler just has very bad manners. Whereas political correctness is really just fascism posing as good manners. When you get a minute, look up the Frankfurt School and you can see how and why the whole charade started. The deliberate intention was to cause chaos in society.'

'Wow, James. I didn't realise you felt so strongly about it!'

'Indeed, I do, Sandy. Every intelligent person should. If you disagree with someone, then destroy their position using rational argument. Not by making them too scared to speak or to laugh or by trying to get them sacked from their job. And while you're at it, look up Voltaire. He had the right idea over two hundred years ago.'

'I'll certainly do that, James.'

Roger, Guy and Dick returned from the gents. Dick made for the door. 'OK folks, I'm off now, certainly nice to meet y'all, particularly all you pretty ladies and oh excuse me, sir.'

Kingsley was filling the doorway and impeding his exit. 'You haven't paid your bar bill yet, Mr Dangler. Forty-two pounds, fifty pence please.' Kingsley held out his hand.

CHAPTER SEVEN

'Well I don't think we will meet Mr Dangler again anytime soon,' said George when Dick had left, 'so boys, you went to the khazi with him. Did he live up to his name?'

'Yes, he certainly did,' said Roger, 'I can only describe it as looking like a baby's arm holding an apple!'

'Steady on,' said Guy, 'you'll make Mandy go weak at the knees. I hear Mandy got halfway to Ireland before she found out a Murphy twenty-two inch was a television.'

'Would you like another bandage for your head, Guy? Hopefully, it'll go round your mouth.'

'Well we couldn't help but stare at it, and he noticed we were looking,' continued

Roger, 'He said it was so large due to his mother only having one arm.'

'How on earth could his mother only having one arm, affect the size of his cock?' asked George.

'Well, because when he was a kid, it was the only way she could lift him out of the bath.'

'A likely story! He didn't like the Ku Klux Klan reference, did he?'

'I'd like to join the Ku Klux Klan,' said Guy, 'but only to find out what detergent they use. I've never seen sheets and pillowcases so white.'

'The hotbed off incest, religion and racism remark seemed to upset him as well.'

'Well, perhaps Mr Dangler would feel more at home staying at the hotel in Molden. Incest is so rife in Molden, the hospital has to order special surgical gloves with six fingers.'

'Well, I've been to the deep south and it seems to match,' said Roger, 'every other building is some sort of church.'

'I know they are very religious all over the states,' said Mandy, 'but over here most people don't even bother to go to church.'

'Can argue with that,' replied Guy, 'the

only church I want to be inside is Charlotte!'

'I have to go now, Roger,' said Mandy.

'OK Mandy, I'll walk you to your car.'

Roger and Mandy left the club. 'Mandy, I've never asked you before but where do you live?'

'Oh, I live in Lower Linton.'

Roger looked puzzled. 'I've never heard of Lower Linton, where exactly is it?'

'Well, to be honest, I live in Fleawick. But just at the bottom of the hill, right on the border with Linton. Fleawick has such a dreadful reputation, I tell everyone the area is actually called Lower Linton.'

'Yes, the industrial estate where Vic from Hell works and the council estate certainly don't help, do they? I knew someone who lived in Fleawick years ago. The house was a tip and absolutely filthy, yet they had doormats at the front and back doors. It puzzled me for a while until I saw them wipe their feet before they went outside. Made perfect sense then.'

Mandy laughed. 'Sounds like one of Kyle's stories.'

'No, this is true. And whenever I've been to the supermarket in Fleawick, I've found the handles on the shopping trolleys so sticky. What on earth these Fleawick women do with their hands to get them so sticky I really can't imagine.'

Mandy got in her car. 'Careful now, you are talking to a Fleawick woman, and you can imagine what they do to get their hands so sticky, unless of course, you've got an extremely short memory!'

'Point taken!' said Roger and gave her a kiss, 'Don't forget to ask Dan whether he is thinking about divorce.'

'I won't. See you next lesson.'

'Bye.'

Mandy drove off, narrowly missing another car as it swung into the car park far too fast. The car pulled up alongside Roger and the driver got out.

'Hello Steve,' said Roger.

'Hello Roger,' replied Steve, 'Pleased to see your black eye is nearly back to normal but if that was the lovely Mandy I saw going out the gate, then perhaps you are looking for another one!'

Roger and Steve walked into the club. Steve made a beeline for George.

'Hello George, I've got some good news,' said Steve, 'I saw Hugh the Customs guy, and he tipped me off the Bonded Store has

28

got the go-ahead to sell duty-free to private pilots on foreign trips. So I've been over there and arranged for me to use it. Strictly cash though.'

'Great news,' said George, 'now we can buy at the same price as the airlines do. Must be a lot cheaper than foreign supermarkets or duty-free shops in airports!'

CHAPTER EIGHT

Roger sidled over to Sandy who was standing with her crew. Kyle spotted him first.

'Ooh watch out Sandy, here comes the Lothario.'

'Thank you, Kyle,' said Roger, 'Sandy, can I get you a G and T now?'

'No thanks, Roger, the crew bus will be here shortly and I don't like to gulp them down.'

'I'll have one Roger, you'd be surprised what I can gulp down,' said Kyle.

'I don't think I would be surprised actually, Kyle,' replied Roger, 'But I hear you had some problems with Customs and Excise recently. Apparently, they found a false bottom in your suitcase?'

Kyle looked outraged. 'Ooh that's slander, that is. Are you suggesting I smuggle drugs or something?'

'No Kyle, a false bottom. A male posterior that wasn't real.'

Kyle's face remained outraged for a moment before the penny dropped, and he burst into laughter. 'Oh, that's brilliant Roger. Did you think of that yourself?'

'Yes,' lied Roger.

'Thanks. I'll add it to my repertoire of funny stories.'

'Come on folks, the crew bus is here,' shouted Captain Slack from the door.

'Bye, Roger,' said Sandy 'I'll have that G and T one day!'

'Bye, Sandy,'

Roger went back to Guy, George and Steve.

'Not got your leg over Sandy yet?' asked Guy.

'Not yet,' replied Roger 'I must ask you for a few tips Guy, now you are our sex guru.'

'Oh, don't take the piss. I just got lucky with Enis, that's all,' confessed Guy, 'I haven't always been so lucky.'

'Really, Guy? You amaze me.'

'I once had a girlfriend who was a bit more sophisticated than me. One night she said "Come round to my place tomorrow night. I have mirrors on my bedroom ceiling and mirrors on my bedroom walls. Bring a bottle!"'

'Sounds perfect!' said George, 'What went wrong?'

'I took Windowlene.'

'You Pillock!'

'Well, I was only young.'

'I've got a mirror in my bedroom,' said Roger.

'What, a big one on the ceiling?'

'No, it's a small one. I hold it under Alison's nose when we're having sex, to see if she's still breathing.'

CHAPTER NINE

'The beer is certainly better today,' remarked George, 'hopefully these two new guys know what they are doing. About time for another round, I think. Steve, your round, where the hell is Steve?'

'I saw him nip out a couple of minutes ago,' said Roger.

'His round and the bugger has run off again. I'll order the drinks, and he can pay when he gets back.'

George lent over the bar. 'Kingsley, can we have four pints down here please.' He turned to Roger.

'So you've passed your Air Law today, which means going solo will be the next milestone. Have you got your medical sorted out?'

Roger looked shocked. 'No, I thought you just needed that before you got your licence.'

'No. You need that before you can go solo. You can't be in charge of an aircraft if you're likely to have a heart attack or something!'

'Oh, I'd better sort that out then. Can I go to my GP?'

'No, you need a specialist CAA approved medical examiner. Luckily, there's one in Fleawick, Dr Mitchell.'

'Right, I'll book an appointment with Dr Mitchell.'

Kingsley placed four pints on the bar. 'Sixteen pounds please.'

'Thanks, Kingsley. It's Steve's round, and he's just nipped to the bog. He'll pay when he gets back.'

Kingsley looked less than pleased. 'OK, but you ordered them, so I'm holding you responsible.'

'Heavens, you are a trusting soul aren't you. Look, here he comes now. Steve, your round I believe. Kingsley needs sixteen pounds.'

'My round again? Are you sure?'

'Yes Steve, I'm very sure! So where have you been?'

'I've been to the toilet.'

'You spend more time in the bloody toilet than George Michael.' said Guy.

'Yes,' said George, 'you go every time it's your round. It wouldn't be that you're a tight bastard and trying to avoid parting with any cash, would it?'

'No.'

'Only someone told me that the only reason you had double glazing fitted in your house was so your kids couldn't hear the ice cream van!'

'That's ridiculous.'

'Is it? What about last week when you dropped that penny. You bent down to pick it up and it hit you on the back of the neck.'

'You're making that up.'

'Am I? If the cap fits, wear it.'

'Time for me to start my disco,' said Guy.

'Oh, that's a shame,' said Roger.

'Why is that?'

'Everybody was just starting to enjoy themselves.'

'I'll ignore that Roger. Catch you later.'

Guy walked over to the stage.

'Good evening, Ladies and Gentlemen. Welcome to the Cloud Nine disco with your host, Prince Charles.'

'I'll start tonight as always by reading

today's main stories from your local rag, the Linton, Fleawick and Moldon Evening Gazette.'

'I see your local pervert has been released from prison after serving just two years of a four-year sentence. Mind you, he always did like half-terms. It was also reported that the first thing he wanted to do was to take his family on holiday. What a stupid newspaper reporter. What he actually said was that he was going to tamper with the kids.'

'Mummy and Daddy, that's the Queen and the Duke of Edinburgh have announced they are going on one last world charm offensive. The Queen will provide the charm and the Duke will be offensive.'

'And I see bigamy is on the rise in China, well that doesn't surprise me. If you have one Chinese wife, you are bound to want another one, half an hour later.'

'So, let's start off tonight with the Rolling Stones and Paint it Black. All you flying types can imagine yourselves in a Huey helicopter flying over Vietnam.'

George looked at Roger and shook his head. 'Roger, you heard me when we were in Le Touquet, didn't you? Get a new scriptwriter Guy, I said. Did he take any notice?'

Roger smiled. 'Apparently not.'

CHAPTER TEN

Roger and Alison were eating breakfast.

'I've passed my Air Law exam,' said Roger, 'it won't be long before I'm going solo.'

'Uh-huh.'

'I need to pass a flying medical first.'

'Uh-huh.'

'I've got an appointment with a flying doctor this afternoon.'

'Going to Wallamboola Base, are you?'

'Ah, it speaks. Not a lot of sense though. Walla—what?'

'Wallamboola Base. When the Flying Doctor used to be on the radio, I seem to remember a lot of "Wallamboola Base, calling Flying Doctor".'

'Not that sort of flying doctor, you idiot.

A doctor who's been specially trained to do medicals on pilots.'

'Uh-huh.'

'I'm seeing one later.'

'Uh-huh.'

'I do wish you would take me learning to fly seriously. You know how much you like the seaside but are always complaining about how the beaches in the UK are full of men with knotted handkerchiefs on their heads? Well, we can fly to Nice or Cannes or Biarritz. You can enjoy the sea with a nicer class of person.'

'You remind me of the sea, Roger.'

'What, you think I'm wild, restless and untamed?'

'No! You make me sick!'

'Charmed I'm sure. I don't understand you, Alison. You've got a nice house, car, job and I think a nice husband who is working hard to broaden our horizons. When I get a pilot's licence, we can fly around Europe and enjoy the high life. I would have thought any woman would be over the moon with the situation and would be all over me like a rash. But instead, you avoid me in the bedroom and prefer having coffee with a Eunuch.'

'Sex, Sex, Sex, that's all you think about Roger. There are other things in life.'

'Yes, and I think I just listed a lot of them a few moments ago. But sex makes the world go around. If God invented anything more enjoyable than sex, she kept it to herself. What on earth is the matter with you?'

'Well since you ask, my job is not going too well. I'm trying hard for promotion but it seems there is a glass ceiling at work when it comes to promoting women.'

'Doesn't make much sense. If there was a glass ceiling at work, surely the men would make sure all the women worked upstairs?'

'There you go again, Roger. Sex, Sex, Sex. Dan's not like that. He values people for what they are, not what they look like or the amount of sex they want.'

'Really? Then I wonder why he married Mandy. Absolutely gorgeous and up for it at every opportunity.'

'Oh, there speaks the man who knows! You are impossible, Roger. I'm off to work.'

Alison got up and slammed the door behind her. BANG!

Oops, thought Roger, *perhaps an admission too far!*

CHAPTER ELEVEN

Roger walked into Flight Training reception. Mandy was manning the desk.

'Hello, Roger.'

'Hello Mandy, how're tricks?'

'I'm not sure, Roger. I asked Dan if he was considering divorce, and he said yes.'

'Oh, so, Alison was telling the truth.'

'Yes. They also had lunch together yesterday. Did you know that?'

'No. I didn't.' She didn't let anything slip this time.'

'Dan said they get on very well together. To be fair though, Dan is a very easy-going person.'

'I imagine that's the attraction for Alison. She likes to manipulate people and get her own way. He sounds a sitting duck. I wonder what he sees in her?'

'It won't be sex. Dan's got a very low sex drive. That has been the main problem in our marriage.'

'In that case, it probably is sex or the potential lack of it. They are well-matched from that point of view. They can lay in bed together and argue about who has the worst headache!'

'Dan has never said he had a headache.'

'So, how did you two get married if you had such different views about sex?'

'Well he seemed OK to start with, but he just seemed to lose interest as time went on. What about you and Alison? I could ask the same question.'

'And I'd give you the same answer. If Dan and Alison are having lunch together secretly, maybe they are planning to divorce us. How do you feel about that?'

'I don't know, Roger. You make me feel alive whereas Dan doesn't, but he is a nice, kind chap. Never violent; well except when being described as a Eunuch. How do you feel about it all?'

'Well, the same as you do, except Alison isn't a nice, kind person. So what do we do?'

'I'm not sure, Roger. Play it by ear, I

suppose. But I'm certainly not running straight home after work if he's been having lunch with your wife. I'd rather stay here and have a drink with you. I think I can probably find some keys to an executive jet if I look —'

'Mandy, can you help me, please?' Lewis came out of his office at speed, 'I've got a maintenance invoice here for changing a Press To Talk switch in Hotel-Tango. They are charging £250 for the Press To Talk switch plus labour. Who authorised it?'

'Mike did before he was sacked. It definitely was faulty as Roger here can verify. It got stuck during one of his lessons and caused a certain amount of merriment.'

'Why merriment?'

'Well, it was the topic of the ongoing conversation in the aircraft when it got stuck. ATC recorded it and spread it around the club.'

'OK, so the switch was faulty, but £250 for a micro switch? They are having a laugh. You can buy those in electronic component shops for £2.50 each. I think they've got the decimal point in the wrong place. I'll send the invoice back.'

Roger laughed. 'Aren't you forgetting the

definition of an aeroplane, Lewis?'

'What do you mean?'

'I thought the definition of an aeroplane was a hole in the sky that pilots pour endless amounts of money into.'

'That may well be Roger, but not my money. Now, are you ready for your lesson?'

'You bet, Lewis.'

'OK Mandy, can you book us out in Hotel-Tango please.'

'Will do, Lewis.'

CHAPTER TWELVE

Hotel-Tango was taxiing toward the holding point for runway two-six.

'Now I want you to do a normal take-off Roger, but when we reach about four hundred feet, I shall simulate an engine failure,' said Lewis, 'I'll take control and show you the procedure. Then we'll complete the circuit and next time around, you will have control and you can follow the procedure yourself. OK?'

'OK.'

Roger reached the holding point. He completed the engine and pre-flight checks. 'Linton Tower, Hotel-Tango, checks complete, ready for departure.'

'Roger, Hotel-Tango. Cleared take off runway two-six, QFE Niner-Niner-Seven,

45

wind calm.'

'Cleared take-off runway two-six, Niner-Niner-Seven, Hotel-Tango.'

Roger taxied on to the runway, opened the throttle and began his take-off run. He rotated and trimmed for the climb.

At four hundred feet, Lewis pressed the PTT button. 'Hotel-Tango, simulated engine failure on take-off.'

'Roger Hotel-Tango, call climbing away.'

'I have control.' Lewis shut the throttle and set carb heat to hot.

'Right the first thing to do is to trim the aircraft for best glide, 65 Knots. Then choose the best open area ahead, that long field there looks good. Now we simulate the crash drills, throttle closed, mixture to idle cut-off, fuel cock and pump off, ignition off, quickly warn the passengers, harnesses tight, unlatch a door. Call Mayday, engine failure. Use flap if necessary to land in the selected field,' said Lewis. He pressed the PTT button. 'Hotel-Tango climbing away.'

'Roger Hotel-Tango, continue circuit.'

'You have control,' said Lewis.

'I have control,' said Roger.

Roger opened the throttle, put the carb heat back to cold and carefully climbed back to a thousand feet downwind.

'Hotel-Tango, downwind.'

'Roger Hotel-Tango, cleared to finals, number one, QFE Niner-Niner-Seven.'

'Cleared to finals, number one, Niner-Niner-Seven, Hotel-Tango.'

Roger started running through the pre-landing checks in his mind. *Brakes are off, undercarriage down and welded, mixture is rich, carb heat to hot.*

He looked over his shoulder and decided to turn base leg. He reduced the throttle to 1700 rpm and turned left. At five hundred feet and almost aligned with the runway, he turned on to final approach.

'Hotel-Tango finals.'

'Roger, Hotel-Tango. Cleared touch and go, runway two-six. QFE Niner-Niner-Seven. Wind calm.'

'Cleared touch and go, two-six, Hotel-Tango.'

As the aircraft landed on the main wheels, he opened the throttle and accelerated down the runway and lifted off. At four hundred feet, Lewis shut the throttle and set the carb heat to hot.

'Tell the tower you're simulating an engine failure.'

'Hotel-Tango, simulated engine failure on take-off.'

'Roger Hotel-Tango, call climbing away.'

Roger trimmed the aircraft for best glide and looked ahead. 'That long field you chose before certainly looks the best.'

He started to run through the crash drill. 'Throttle closed, mixture to idle cut-off, fuel cock and pump off, ignition off, quickly warn the passengers, harnesses tight, unlatch a door. Call Mayday, engine failure.'

'Hotel-Tango climbing away.'

'Roger Hotel-Tango, continue circuit.'

'Well done, Roger,' said Lewis, 'Never turn back to the airfield. In some circumstances, you may make it, but most of the time you won't as you'll lose so much height in the turn.'

'What do I do if it happens at night?'

'If it happens at night, switch the landing light on at two hundred feet. If you don't like what you see, switch it off again and pray!'

CHAPTER THIRTEEN

Roger walked into the club, expecting to find either Kingsley or Fidel behind the bar.

'Good afternoon, sir,' said a well-spoken voice, 'what can I get you?'

Roger looked up and saw a well-dressed, rather portly man standing at the end of the bar.

'Oh hello, pint of bitter please.'

'Certainly sir.'

'Are Kingsley or Fidel about?' asked Roger.

'No, sir,' came the reply, 'Not for a couple of days, I'm afraid. They are away on business arranging the beer and food supplies.'

'You would have thought one would have gone away while the other one stays here to run the bar.'

'Well, I'm afraid they are inseparable. They've been together for many years.'

'Oh, right. Together as in the biblical sense. No wonder he didn't like it when I called him Fiddle!'

'Anyway, I'm here to serve you. I'm Piers.'

'Pleased to meet you, Piers. I'm Roger.'

'Pleased to meet you, Roger. I'll be standing in for the boys when they can't be here.'

'Have you worked for them for long?'

'No, but they were looking for an experienced barman that would match their plans for this club. I used to be a sommelier at a smart restaurant in town. I do cocktails as well. My Piers-Buster was quite famous in the Club Bar at The Waldorf Hotel.'

'Then you'll definitely be an improvement on Chantelle.'

'Who is Chantelle?'

'She was a teenage know nothing barmaid on minimum wage. Hopeless as a barmaid, but slightly better as a bouncer.'

'What happened to her?'

'She got sacked the other night. Six people were arrested in here for fighting. Unfair, as she did try to break the fight up.'

'Oh, I thought Kingsley said this was a nice quiet place with just pilots and crew.'

'Yes, that was what he was led to believe before he signed the contract. Unfortunately, the owner has a late licence, and he has opened the club up to all the local arseholes. That's where the trouble comes from.'

'Well, I know Kingsley and Fidel have great plans for this club. A range of real ales from different breweries and delicious home-cooked food. Kingsley is a great chef. But for all that to succeed, they require intelligent and sophisticated customers.'

'I'm sure the crews will appreciate it but I don't think Vic from Hell will. All he and his mates will want is lager and pies.'

'Vic from Hell?'

'Vic from Hull really, but Hell is more suitable for him. He cleans out the Portaloos on their return from building sites.'

Piers pulled a face. 'Sounds ghastly.'

'Which, Vic or what he does?'

'Both!'

'So, Piers, tell me. What are those workmen doing to the window between the two bars?'

'They are just putting some shelves in, and a hinged glass door.'

'Yes, I can see that, but why?'

'Because that will be the boys "Cabinet of Curiosities", that's why.'

'What on earth is a cabinet of curiosities?'

'Well, it's something the boys have been collecting for a long while. It goes with them wherever they go.'

'Yes, but what is it?'

'Oh, I'm afraid you'll just have to wait until it's finished.'

CHAPTER FOURTEEN

'Hello Roger, how's your belly off for spots?'

'Oh hello, Kyle. No crew with you today?'

'No, not today. No Sandy for you to chat up, I'm afraid.'

'Day off, is it?'

'Yes, we don't work seven days a week, you know. I've just popped in for a quick one.'

'I'll assume you are talking about a drink.'

'Well not necessarily, Roger. I'm a Martini type of guy.'

'Martini guy?'

'Yes, as in any time, any place, anywhere. Remember the advert? How about you?'

'Sorry, Kyle. I only drink from the furry

cup. I do not drop anchor in Pooh bay.'

'Oh, shame! Well, nothing ventured, nothing gained. I'll leave you in peace.'

'No hard feelings?'

'I know. You made that bit crystal clear.'

'I didn't mean that you idiot! Now, any more stories for me?'

'Well before I joined this crew, I was on another one and the pilot was a bit of a wag. Soon after we took off he used to say things like "smoking in the toilets is prohibited and anyone caught will be asked to leave the aircraft immediately" and when we were coming into land at night he would say "I'm turning down the cabin lights for your comfort and to enhance the appearance of the cabin crew". Quite the joker.'

Roger laughed. 'He sounds like fun. I can't imagine James Slack saying things like that.'

'Oh no. James is strictly by the book. Thoroughly nice man though. Anyway, don't do anything I wouldn't do. Bye.'

The world is my oyster then thought Roger.

He looked around the bar and noticed Miles and another man sitting by themselves. He walked over.

'Hello Miles, you said you'd be back later

in the week and here you are,'

'Hello Roger, pleased to see the shiner has all but disappeared. Roger, I'd like you to meet Owen, he's a colleague from Thailand. Owen, this is Roger, he's learning to fly.'

'Pleased to meet you, Roger,' said Owen, 'I'd give up the flying now, mate. You'll never make any money at it.'

'Nice to meet you too, Owen. But I only ever intend to fly for fun, not money.'

'That's what I said, Roger. Next thing I know, I'm in the Fleet Air Arm flying jets on an aircraft carrier at night.'

'Wow, That sounds exciting, Owen.'

'It is exhilarating, Roger. The three best things in life are a good landing, a good orgasm and a good shit. Landing on a carrier at night is one of the few opportunities to have all three at the same time!'

Roger laughed. 'Yes, I can see that. So presumably you're not doing that in Thailand now?'

'Oh no. I fly helicopters for the same outfit Miles is with. Flying people out to oil rigs and the like. I came back on the same flight as Miles but I had a bit of business in Wales to attend to. I've only just got back to

Linton.'

'I thought the only good things to come out of Wales were rugby players and loose women,' said Roger.

'Hey, do you mind, Roger, my wife comes from Wales.'

'Really?' said Roger, thinking quickly, 'What position does she play?'

CHAPTER FIFTEEN

Roger was on his way back to the bar for another drink as George came walked in. 'Hello Roger. How did the flying medical go? Did you pass?'

'I'm not sure,' said Roger, 'he did most of the tests this afternoon and didn't seem too bothered, but when it came to the urine test I found I couldn't go. So he gave me a urine test to take away and do.'

'Have you done it yet?'

'Yes. He stressed it was important to do it mid-stream. Well, what those poor fishermen must have thought of me, I can't imagine. Look, my trousers are still wet. Anyway, I'll take it back tomorrow and get the result.'

'Yes, they do ask you some funny things

in those medicals.'

'Indeed. He asked me how often I had sex. I said infrequently. He thought about it for a moment and asked was that one word or two. It's one word, I said. You obviously don't know my wife!'

'I remember Dr Mitchell's hearing test. He would say "put your hand over your right ear" and he would whisper "what's your name?". I would tell him, and then he would say "put your hand over your left ear" and whisper again "what's your name?". I used to laugh and say I just told you. Didn't you hear? And you're the one testing my hearing?'

Roger laughed. 'He said he would need samples of my faeces, semen and urine. I said no problem, I'll leave my underpants behind.'

'Well, let's hope it all goes well for you tomorrow. At least there are witnesses to prove you did it mid-stream!' said George, 'Now, I was hoping to catch you today. Steve and I are planning our next flight, are you interested in participating?'

'Yes, I'd love to. Where are you going?'
'Jernsey.'
'Jernsey? Where the hell is that?'

'The Channel Isles. Jersey or Guernsey. Could be either, so we call it Jernsey.'

'Yes, sounds brilliant. I've never been to the Channel Isles. Count me in. Not sure about Mandy though.'

'Well, you can work that one out with her. I suppose it depends on whether you want another black eye.'

'I'd punch him straight back if he tried that again. He's been having lunch with my wife.'

'Just lunch, eh? Well, that seems a pretty good deal, considering what you've been doing with his wife!'

'So, what's the route to Jernsey from here?'

'Straight down to Southampton via Basingswick, then straight past The Needles to Cap de la Hague for Jersey, or to the Casquets Lighthouse for Guernsey.'

'Is Basingswick a bit like Jernsey?'

'Yes, it's our pet name for Basingstoke.'

'OK, that's what I thought. I won't ask why. Yes, that route sort of fits in my head. Is there much to do there?'

'Oh yes, loads. We normally go for lunch at one of the many good restaurants, like the Lobster Pot, and drive around the island afterwards. So much to see. We even bumped into John Nettles once.'

'He was playing Bergerac, I suppose. John Nettles, the Stinging Detective!'

'Both Jersey and Guernsey have traditional fish markets. I think I mentioned to you on the Le Touquet trip we often bring crabs and lobsters back with us. When we go to the local Chinky restaurant on our return, Ken and Suzy Wong make some wonderful dishes for us.'

'Yes George, you did mention it but unfortunately, I was nursing a black eye soon after we landed. I'm really looking forward to trying the food this time.'

'There's a lot of bunkers as well. The Germans occupied the islands during the war and turned the place into a fortress. There's an underground hospital and lots of the smaller bunkers have been restored by the locals.'

'It all sounds very interesting, George.'

CHAPTER SIXTEEN

'Ah, here comes Mandy,' said Roger, 'Would you like a drink, Mandy?'

'I'll have a G and T please.'

'Piers, can I have a G and T and two pints of bitter, please.'

He turned to Mandy, 'Mandy, I've just been discussing a forthcoming trip to the Channel Isles with George. Are you interested?'

'I'm not sure, Roger. You know I would love to, but not rushing home at night is one thing, going out with you for a whole day is something quite different.'

'OK, well bear it in mind, and we'll see how things progress.'

Guy walked into the club carrying some records under his arm. He spotted Roger,

Mandy and George and came over.

'Hello, who is the new chap behind the bar?'

'That's Piers. He's looking after the bar as Kingsley and Fiddle have gone away on business. He seems to be an excellent barman.'

'Oh, right,' said Guy 'Can I get you three a drink?'

'No, thanks, Guy,' said Roger, 'we've just got one.'

Guy went to the bar. 'Hello Piers. I'm Guy. I do the disco. Can I have a pint of bitter please.'

'Good evening, Guy,' replied Piers, glancing at the bar clock. 'I've been expecting you. Aren't you cutting it a bit fine?'

'Not at all, Piers, I'm ready to start straight away.'

Guy picked up his pint and walked over to the stage.

'Good evening, Ladies and Gentlemen. Welcome to the Cloud Nine disco with your host, Prince Charles.'

'I'll start tonight as always by reading today's main stories from your local rag, the Linton, Fleawick and Moldon Evening

Gazette.'

'I see our local MP has revealed that she got stung by a bee the other day. Yes, twelve pounds for a small jar of honey.'

'Sarah Ferguson has just had a big reunion, apparently her knees are back together again after all this time.'

'And the boiling hot weather in Linton continues. I've noticed lots of young ladies walking around in very short skirts and skimpy tops. It rose as high as ninety degrees last week, and that's not bad for a man of my age, I can tell you!'

'So let's remain on that theme and start this evening with Summer Nights from the musical Grease.'

Roger lent over to Mandy. 'Time to go, I think.'

CHAPTER SEVENTEEN

Roger and Mandy walked outside the club.

'Have you got the keys?' asked Roger.

'Yes, have you got the blanket?' replied Mandy.

'We can collect it from my car on the way past.'

'It's a bit light still. I hope no one notices us.'

Roger collected the blanket from his boot, and they walked through the perimeter fence to the executive jet.

Mandy unlocked the door, and they went inside.

Roger spread the blanket on the floor, and they both laid on it.

'Oh, this is so nice,' said Mandy.

'This aircraft is the only place I have sex, these days,' said Roger. He kissed Mandy and began to undress her.

She responded by tearing at his clothes.

A while later, Mandy heard a noise. 'What's that noise?'

'What noise?'

'Sounds like footsteps.'

'I can't hear any —'

Suddenly, the door opened and there stood Mr Hamilton. 'What the hell is going on? Oh, is that you Mandy??'

Roger got off Mandy and reached for his trousers, but was unable to stop his erection wobbling from side to side like an over wound metronome.

'Oh, my good Lord,' said Mr Hamilton, turning his back, 'sort yourselves out and I'll see you both outside.' He shut the door.

Mandy scrabbled around on the floor looking for her underwear, 'Oh no, if he complains to the club, I'll lose my job.'

'How embarrassing.'

They both got dressed and then looked at each other in horror.

'What on earth are we going to say to him?' asked Mandy.

'I really don't know,' said Roger, 'I just

hope he doesn't put two and two together and realise why he had a damp carpet. Are you ready?'

'Yes, I think so.'

Mandy opened the door, and they both stepped out of the aircraft. Mandy locked it behind her.

'Well, what have you got to say for yourselves,' asked Mr Hamilton.

Mandy looked at the ground. 'I'm so sorry, Mr Hamilton.'

'I should think so. I left that key with the club in case of emergencies, not so you could use the bloody aircraft as a knocking-shop. What will happen if I complain to the club tomorrow?'

'I'll lose my job,' whimpered Mandy, 'Please don't do that.'

'Now I know what's been going on, it's not difficult to work out why I had the problem with the damp carpet is it?'

'No, Mr Hamilton.'

'It cost me a hundred and fifty pounds for an engineer to strip the cabin looking for a leak. Now I'm looking at what was leaking.' He turned to Roger. 'Well, you're very quiet, letting Mandy take all the flak. What have you got to say for yourself?'

'Yes, well I'm sorry too. Please don't complain to the club. Mandy loves her job. We are both having problems with our spouses and this is how we are getting through it. You are right about the leak. We both felt bad about that which is why I bring this blanket now. I'm happy to reimburse the cost of the engineer if you can just keep Mandy's name out of it. Surely, at some point in your life, you must have done something similar?'

Mr Hamilton laughed. 'Ten out of ten for sticking up for Mandy and ten out of ten for cheek! But yes, you're right, I suppose. But it wasn't in someone else's executive jet. How are you going to pay?'

Roger reached in his back pocket and got his wallet out. 'Is cash OK?'

CHAPTER EIGHTEEN

Roger and Alison were eating breakfast.

'I've just got to drop this urine test into the doctor and if it tests OK he should issue my medical certificate.'

'Uh-huh.'

'That means I can go solo when the instructor thinks I'm ready.'

'Uh-huh.'

'You are still not taking this —'

Alison's mobile phone started to ring. As something flashed up on the screen, she looked at it in horror, picked it up and rushed out into the garden.

Roger continued to tuck into his toast. Through the window, he watched Alison walking up and down the garden path, talking into her phone.

After a minute or so, Alison came back in. She gave Roger a black look.

'What's up?', asked Roger, 'work problem?'

'No,' said Alison, 'Husband problem!'

Roger looked puzzled. 'What?'

'That was Dan. He said Mandy got home a bit later than usual last night and seemed upset about something. When they went to bed, he noticed her underwear was on inside out and back to front, again!'

Roger went white but quickly composed himself. 'Yes, and?'

Alison narrowed her eyes. 'I told him you were at the club last night, and he wondered if you saw her with anyone?'

Roger breathed a bit easier. 'I remember she was in the bar briefly, but then I think she said she was going home. I didn't notice her leave with anyone.'

'If I find out you've been seeing her again Roger, I'll —'

'Whoa, whoa, not so fast. What about these cosy lunches you've been having with Dan?'

It was Alison's turn to look shocked. She said nothing.

'Oh, so not so pious now. Nothing to

say?'

'There is nothing to say, Roger. We've met for lunch but only to discuss you and Mandy.'

'That must take all of thirty seconds and be pretty boring. What do you talk about after you've ordered your food?'

'We're not having sex if that's what you think.'

'Good grief, that's the last thing I would think! Fleawick's Chief Eunuch has lunch with Linton's Mother Superior, hardly Lady Chatterley stuff is it?'

'Oh, you are impossible, Roger. I'm going to work.'

Alison got up and slammed the door behind her. BANG!

CHAPTER NINETEEN

Roger walked into the Flight Training reception with a big smile on his face.

'Hello, Mandy, great news, I've passed my pilot medical.'

Mandy was less than enthusiastic. 'That's good.'

'Sorry Mandy, I was so pleased about my medical I forgot Dan had noticed your underwear malfunction again.'

'How on earth do you know about that?'

'Dan phoned Alison this morning to tell her, and she gave me the third degree.'

'What did you tell her?'

'Nothing. But I did catch her out about having lunches with Dan. She says they only meet to discuss us, oh, and they're not having sex.'

71

'I didn't think that was likely anyway.'

'Me neither. Apparently, Dan said you seemed upset about something when you got home?'

'Upset? I'm absolutely traumatised by what happened last night. I've never been so embarrassed in all my life.'

'Yes, it was embarrassing but look on the bright side. Mr Hamilton won't say anything to the club, so your job is safe.'

'Yes, thanks for sorting that out. If I had lost my job and the reason had come out, I don't think I could have looked anyone in the eye ever again.'

Lewis's office door opened and Lewis and Jane emerged.

'Bye darling,' said Jane and kissed him on the lips.

'Bye darling,' replied Lewis.

Jane turned and walked straight past Roger and Mandy without acknowledging them.

'Hello Roger,' said Lewis, 'Did you pass your medical?'

'Yes,' said Roger, 'I dropped the urine sample into Dr Mitchell this morning, he tested it and issued my certificate.'

'Oh well done, Roger. So have you got the

medical certificate with you?'

Roger nodded and handed it to Lewis.

'Mandy, can you photocopy it and put the copy into Roger's record please. Roger, I'll be with you in a minute. I've just got to ring the tower, then we'll go and bash the circuit.'

Lewis disappeared back into his office and shut the door.

Mandy scowled. 'I can't stand those two. They're always drooling over each other.'

'Oh, I think they make a fastidious couple,' said Roger.

'Really? Why?'

'Because he's fast, and she's hideous!'

CHAPTER TWENTY

'Hotel-Tango finals,' said Roger.

'Roger Hotel-Tango, you're number one, cleared land or touch and go at your discretion.'

'Say Hotel-Tango landing,' said Lewis.

'Hotel-Tango landing,' said Roger. He looked at Lewis, 'Why, we've only been airborne twenty minutes.'

'Just concentrate on your landing,' said Lewis, 'I thought you had forgotten I was here. That's the first thing you've said to me since we got in the bloody aeroplane.'

Roger landed the aircraft on the numbers and continued down the runway.

'Pull in to the taxiway there,' said Lewis, 'I'm going back to the club. Go and do one more circuit, land and taxi back to the club.

Make sure you shut everything down as per checklist. The guy in the tower knows exactly what is happening. I'll see you later.'

And with that, Lewis got out of the aircraft and walked off.

Oh shit thought Roger. He looked apprehensively at the empty seat next to him. Then he realised that this was what he had been wanting to do all his life.

He pressed the PTT button. 'Linton Tower, Hotel-Tango, request taxi for one circuit and landing.'

'Hotel-Tango, Linton Tower. Hello Roger, PTT switch Malcolm here. The airfield is yours. Cleared to taxi back down the runway, turn and take off runway two-six. QFE one-zero-one-one, Wind two-seven-zero at five knots. Good luck.'

'Cleared taxi back and take off runway two-six. QFE one-zero-one-one. Hotel-Tango. Thanks, Malcolm.'

'And Roger, if the PTT switch should stick, continue the circuit and land. I'll make sure nothing gets in your way.'

'Thanks, Malcolm. I'll never live that down, will I?'

Roger opened the throttle, turned and taxied back down the runway. He reached the end, turned and lined up. He ran through the checklist in his mind.

Flaps up, carb heat cold, mixture rich, fuel on, one-zero-one-one set on the subscale of the altimeter.

Roger pushed the throttle forward and commenced his takeoff run. At sixty five knots, he pulled back on the control column and became airborne.

He climbed to five hundred feet and commenced a climbing turn to the left. At one thousand feet, he turned left again and held the aircraft's nose down until the speed was ninety knots. He pulled the throttle back to 2200 rpm and trimmed the aircraft for level flight.

'Hotel-Tango downwind.'

'Roger, Hotel-Tango. Cleared to finals, number one.'

'Cleared to finals, number one. Hotel-Tango.'

Roger started running through the pre-landing checks in his mind.

Brakes are off, undercarriage down and welded, mixture is rich, carb heat to hot.

He looked over his shoulder and decided to turn base leg. He reduced the throttle to 1700 rpm and turned left. At five hundred feet and almost aligned with the runway, he turned on to final approach.

'Hotel-Tango finals.'

'Roger, Hotel-Tango. Cleared to land runway two-six. QFE one-zero-one-one. Wind calm.'

'Cleared land, two-six, Hotel-Tango.'

Roger kept the speed at around 65 Kts with the elevators, and controlled the rate of descent with the throttle. As he passed over the threshold, he reduced the power slightly and pulled back gently on the control column.

As the aircraft landed on the main wheels, Roger shut the throttle, applied the brakes and let the aircraft run towards the taxiway back to the club. As he turned on to the taxiway, a round of applause came over the radio.

'Well done, Roger. I'll be at the club later and I'll buy you a drink.'

'Thanks, Malcolm, but the drinks tonight are all on me!'

'OK, make sure you shut the aeroplane down properly. Don't spoil the occasion.'

'Will do!'

Roger taxied Hotel-Tango back to the club. He found his checklist and went

through the shutdown procedure
methodically.

He got out of the aircraft and locked the
door, walked through the perimeter fence
and back to the Flight Training Centre.
Walked? He was flying.

Roger walked through the door but
reception was empty. No Mandy, no Lewis.

Strange thought Roger. He sat down.

Suddenly, there was a bang and the door
to Lewis's office flew open and out rushed
Mandy, Lewis, Guy and George.

Mandy ran up to him and threw her arms
around his neck. 'Well done, Roger. I knew
you could do it!'

Lewis shook his hand. George and Guy
picked him up and said, 'To the bar!'

'I'll join you as soon as I finish here,' said
Mandy.

CHAPTER TWENTY-ONE

Captain Slack and his crew watched in amusement as Roger entered the bar on George and Guys' shoulders.

'OK, Piers. The drinks are on me.'

Sandy came over to the bar. 'What's all this in aid of Roger?'

'Hello, Sandy. I've just gone solo, in an aeroplane that is.'

'Oh, well done Roger. I'm pleased for you!'

'Would you like a G and T now?'

'Yes, please.'

'Can you find out what the rest of your crew would like?'

'That's very kind of you, Roger. I'll go and ask.'

'So Piers, can we have three pints and a G

and T to start with, please.'

'Certainly, Roger. If you are paying for all the drinks tonight, can I ask you to put some money behind the bar and I'll keep track of it for you.'

Roger got his wallet out and passed a wad of notes across the bar. 'Thank you, Piers. Don't forget to include yourself.'

'Thanks, Roger.'

Sandy returned with the crew's order. 'An additional three pints and two G and T's please.'

'I've got it,' said Piers.

Captain Slack came over. 'Roger, I hear congratulations are in order, old boy. Well done!'

'Thanks, James.'

'Well, if you really enjoy flying, Roger, keep on learning. I've done it all my life. I can even remember when flying was dangerous and sex was safe. Funny how things turn around, eh?'

Roger laughed. 'Any words of wisdom for me to remember when flying?'

'Oh lots and lots, Roger,' replied James, 'Here's one. Superior pilots are those that use their superior judgement to avoid situations that may require them to use their superior skill.'

'Thanks, I'll remember that.'

'And here's another, Roger. It's much better to be down here wishing you were up there than it is to be up there wishing you were down here.'

'Thanks again, James. Makes sense. I'll etch both into my memory.'

'And here are the three most useless things in flying. Height above you, runway behind you and fuel still in the bloody bowser.'

Sandy interrupted. 'James, can you help me with these drinks please?'

'Will do, Sandy. Thanks again, Roger.'

'My pleasure James. And thank you for the advice.'

As James and Sandy sat down, Kyle got up and came over. 'Thanks for the drink, Roger.'

'My pleasure, Kyle,' said Roger, 'got any new stories for me?'

'Well, now you come to mention it,' said Kyle, 'I was trying to explain the ditching procedure to a chap on a flight to Shagaluf in Majorca. I told him it was important to get his head right down between his legs. He said if he could do that, he wouldn't

need to go to Shagaluf in the first place.
He'd never leave home again.'

Roger laughed. 'Thanks for that, Kyle.'

'See you, see you, wouldn't want to be you,' said Kyle, and minced off.

CHAPTER TWENTY-TWO

Mandy came into the bar.

'Right Mandy, what would you like to drink?' asked Roger.

'I'll have a G and T please.'

'G and T please, Piers.'

'Well done today, Roger. Lewis was saying he thought you would make an excellent pilot.'

Piers placed a G and T on the bar. Mandy picked it up and raised it in the air.

'Here's to Roger and his flying. He passed an important milestone today. Join me in wishing him many more milestones.'

Everyone raised their glasses. 'To Roger's flying.'

Mandy tipped her head back and took a good mouthful of her G and T.

'Ah here's the lovely Mandy,' said Guy, 'doing what she does best.'

'What do you mean?' asked Mandy.

'Downing shorts. They're normally men's shorts though.'

Mandy stuck her tongue out at Guy but said nothing.

Roger turned to George. 'I meant to ask you when we went to Le Touquet, George, what happens if the engine fails over the sea?'

'We get wet,' said George, 'I showed you the life jackets on the last trip, but we also have a six-man dingy behind the rear seats. As with the life jackets, for heaven's sake don't inflate it until it's outside the aircraft!'

'Oh, I wouldn't want to come down in the sea,' said Mandy, 'a shark might eat me whole!'

'I'm pretty sure it would spit that bit out,' said Guy, 'probably doesn't taste very nice.'

Mandy took a swipe at Guy but he ducked.

'Our bodies might never be found,' continued Mandy, looking daggers at Guy. 'They'd be at the mercy of the currents. I remember Robert Maxwell fell off his yacht in the Canary Isles. His body drifted miles.'

'He didn't fall off his yacht,' said Guy, 'he had an Irish prostitute on-board with him that night. They were smooching on the rear deck, and he said to her "OK, you can toss me off now." So she did.'

'Oh Guy, you really do talk some shit, don't you!' said Mandy angrily.

'No swearing please!' said Piers from behind the bar. He looked straight at Mandy. 'A lady should only swear if it slips out.'

'Oh, and I do swear if it slips out,' said Mandy with a smile, 'luckily that doesn't happen very often.'

'And do you remember the Marie Celeste?' continued Roger, 'They never found any of the crew's bodies. The ship was found floating with nobody on board and all the tables set for dinner.'

'Ah yes, but that was explained,' said Mandy, 'they found one of the dinner menus and Guy was down to do the evening disco.'

Everybody laughed, except Guy. 'Now who's talking —,' he looked across at Piers, who was busy serving somebody '— a load of shit.'

'I heard that Guy!' shouted Piers.

CHAPTER TWENTY-THREE

'Well done, Roger.'

Roger turned and there was Malcolm. 'Malcolm, thank you for your good service this afternoon.'

'My pleasure Roger. Can I buy you a drink?'

'No thanks, Malcolm. I'm celebrating so there's a float behind the bar, just order yourself a drink.'

'Thanks, Roger.'

Malcolm lent over the bar, 'Pint of bitter, please.'

'I've been thinking about your stuck button and your before and after scenarios.'

'Nobody is ever going to let me forget that incident, are they?'

'Well, it's an interesting line of thought.

Now, what if she was a red-headed girl? Before, it would look like a jewel in a copper case, and afterwards it would look like a ginger tom with its throat cut.'

Roger laughed. 'You really do get bored up in the tower, don't you?'

'Well, we've been discussing it in quiet moments. That was the best we could come up with.'

'So Guy, where is Enis?' asked Roger, 'I haven't seen her for a few days. Is she allowing time for your head to heal up before another steamy session?'

'No, she's moved in with me, but she's been on a tattoo course in London and hasn't been getting back until late. You've usually all gone by then. But you're in luck tonight because the course has finished and I'm expecting her anytime soon.'

'Tattoo course? Is that what she does for a living?'

'Yes, it is. She has this brilliant tattoo of a conch shell, right at the top of her left thigh. It's amazing. If you put your ear down to listen to it, I swear you can actually smell the sea.'

'Moved in, eh? I do hope you're being careful, you don't want to get the poor girl pregnant.'

'Oh no, it's fine. She's got one of those coils fitted.'

'My wife had one of those things fitted when we first got married,' said George, 'trouble was, we lived opposite a taxi firm and all you could hear on a Saturday night were things like "pick up Mrs Brown from the Dog and Duck". Kept us awake.'

'Too much information,' said Mandy, 'Now George, I enjoyed the Le Touquet trip so much. Are all your trips that much fun?'

'Oh yes, something always happens to make them memorable. We were in Kinsale in Ireland once, all desperate for a beer. We went into a bar, and the manager rushed over and said "I'm terribly sorry, we don't open for another hour but you're welcome to sit down and have a drink while you are waiting"'

'That's Irish logic, I think.'

'Yes, I think so. When the bar did open, the barman had eyes that looked in opposite directions. When he asked what can I get you, everyone at the bar answered because you couldn't work out who he was talking to. We called him Isaiah, on account of one eye being higher than the other.'

'We had an Irish pilot call us who wanted to divert into Linton as he was short of fuel,' said Malcolm, 'when I asked for his height and position, he said he was six foot and sitting at the front.'

They all laughed.

'On another trip to Ireland, we landed a bit late one evening in Kilkenney,' said George, 'As we walked down the road, a man went by on a tractor. When I asked him what time the pubs shut, he said September!'

'Yes the Irish are a law unto themselves,' said Mandy, 'you never know if they're being serious or not. Unless it comes to religion, and then they are very serious.'

'Yes they are,' agreed Guy, 'A priest once told me he was surprised that Jesus Christ himself didn't choose to be born in Ireland. But as I pointed out, it would have been far too difficult to find three wise men and a virgin.'

CHAPTER TWENTY-FOUR

Enis came into the bar, closely followed by Vic from Hell and some friends.

'Do you still want cock, love?' said Vic.

'Go away, horrible man,' said Enis and made a bee-line for Guy, 'Guy, this man is being very rude.'

'Oh no, it's Vic from Hell,' said Guy, 'weren't you arrested for fighting in here some nights ago?'

'I was but it was all a mistake. Total misunderstanding, and they let us all go same night.'

'Is this man bothering you?' Piers had left the bar and followed Vic over.

'Ooo the hell are you?' asked Vic.

'I'm running this bar at the moment,' said Piers in an authoritative voice, 'I heard what you said to the lady as you came in. If I hear any repeat of that sort of behaviour, you'll be out and your membership revoked. Do I make myself clear?'

Vic was taken aback. 'Crystal mate.'

'Right, we'll say no more about it,' said Piers and returned to the bar.

'Bloody hell,' said Vic, 'is he Lord Muck or something?'

'Lord Piers, perhaps,' said Guy, 'now why don't you go and join your friends at the bar, in case they forget to order you a drink?'

At that, Vic turned and shot off to the bar.

'Brilliant, Guy,' said Roger, 'I didn't think we'd be rid of him so easily.'

'Well, I figured the thought of him missing out on alcohol might be enough.'

'Hello Enis,' said George, 'how are you doing?'

'I am fine George. I am looking forward to trip to Jernsey. Guy tell me all about your trips.'

'Oh I'm sure we'll have some fun, we normally do.'

'Mandy, are you coming on trip to Jernsey?'

'I'm not sure yet.'

'Where is Jernsey, George? I have not heard of it.'

'It's actually called Jersey and it's one of the Channel Isles, near France. Guernsey is another island, so we collectively know them as Jernsey.'

'OK, I think I understand. English madness?'

'Quite probably. So what have you been doing? Guy mentioned tattoos?'

'Yes, I am a tattooist and have been on a course in London. That is now finished. Since I move in with Guy, I have been working to tidy his jungle, or garden as he calls it. It is complete mess. His house is also a mess, with rubbish on every step of his stairs.'

'Are you not a gardener then Guy?' asked Roger.

'No, not since I got arrested for flashing,' said Guy.

'You got arrested for flashing? What, while gardening?'

'Yes. But as I told the policeman, I'm just following the instructions on this pack of seeds. It says prick out every two feet.'

'Sounds like you have your work cut out for you there Enis. Good luck.'

'Yes,' said Enis, 'I need it. You won't believe the time I spent yesterday morning, trimming Guy's front bush.'

CHAPTER TWENTY-FIVE

'I think I better go and start my disco now,' said Guy.

'OK, thanks for the warning,' said Roger.

'Oh Lord, is it that time already?' said George.

'About time I went home, I think,' said Mandy.

'Why you all so nasty about Guy's disco?' asked Enis, 'I think it very good. I give Guy clap every night when he finish.'

She grabbed Guy by the arm, and they went over to the stage.

'I hope that's just her poor English,' said Roger, 'otherwise a condom would be a safer form of contraception than a coil.'

Over on the stage, Guy commenced his disco.

'Good evening, Ladies and Gentlemen. Welcome to the Cloud Nine disco with your host, Prince Charles.'

'I'll start tonight as always by reading today's main stories from your local rag, the Linton, Fleawick and Moldon Evening Gazette.'

'It says here the family planning association is not very pleased. Apparently sperm donations have been hitting the roof.'

'Apple has responded to criticism that many of their products such as the iPhone, the iPad and the iPod are clearly aimed at men, by bringing out a product especially for women. It's called the iRon.'

'And finally, Monica Lewinsky reveals she has just written a book about her affair with Bill Clinton. Well, they do say if you're going to write a book, you should write about the first thing that comes into your head.'

'Now my good friend Roger Moore has done his first solo today, congratulations Roger. So to celebrate, I'll start off tonight with, no, no, come back everyone, no not Cliff Richard's Congratulations, but with Learning To Fly by Tom Petty and the Heartbreakers.'

As the music started to play, Mandy looked at her watch. 'Time to go I think, Roger.'

'OK, I'll see you to your car.'

They walked out into the car park. Luckily Mandy had parked in a quiet corner, so Roger grabbed her and pressed her up against the side of her car and kissed her.

'Oh Roger, what's digging in my stomach?'

'Is that your entry for the stupidest question of the year award, Mandy?'

CHAPTER TWENTY-SIX

Roger and Alison were eating breakfast. Alison was reading a newspaper.

'I did my first solo yesterday.'

'Uh-huh.'

'Just one circuit, taking off, flying around and landing again.'

'Uh-huh.'

'No one else in the aircraft.'

'Uh-huh.'

'Only me.'

'Uh-huh.'

'The instructor had got out and gone back to the club.'

'Uh-huh.'

'I had to deal with air traffic control and everything.'

'Uh-huh.'

'I thought you might be a little more interested, considering your husband flew an aircraft all on his own, for the first time.'

'I am, I've been scrutinising the newspaper to check if there's an announcement in there, but I couldn't see one.'

'Ha bloody ha. So are you seeing the Eunuch for lunch today?'

Alison didn't answer and continued to read the newspaper.

'I'll take that as a yes then. Tell you what, why don't we make it a foursome? I would love to join you and I'm sure Mandy would love to as well.'

'Well, I'm sure you know all about what Mandy loves.'

'So who pays when you go out to lunch? You or the Eunuch?'

Again, Alison didn't answer and continued to read the newspaper.

'So obviously you pay. Now I don't actually know what Dan does for a living.'

'Has your Floozie not told you?'

'We've never had any reason to discuss it. He gave me a black eye, so I'd guess maybe he's an amateur boxer?'

'No. Ask your Floozie.'

'So you pay for his company. When a man pays for a woman's company, that's called prostitution. I wonder if it's the same the other way round?'

'We share the cost of lunch, Roger. But with your obsession with sex, it wouldn't surprise me if you hadn't been with prostitutes!'

'Why on earth would I pay to have sex with someone that despises me, and only does it for the money. Until recently, I got all that at home.'

'Oh, you really are impossible, Roger. I'm off to work.'

Alison got up and slammed the door behind her. BANG!

Give my regards to Dan at lunchtime thought Roger.

CHAPTER TWENTY-SEVEN

Roger walked into the Flight Training reception. Mandy was behind the counter.

'Hello Mandy, how're tricks?'

'Much the same, Roger. How about you?'

'Well, we've just had our usual morning argument, she stormed out and slammed the door again, so much the same as well.'

'What were you arguing about today?'

'The usual. Her having lunch with Dan. I said we'd join them if they liked the idea.'

'Oh, I wouldn't want to do that.'

'You've never told me what does Dan do for a living?'

'Haven't I? He's a gynaecologist, works at the hospital in Moldon.'

'A gynaecologist? Really?'

'Yes.'

'Well, that answers a few questions. When he punched me, I noticed he was wearing his watch above his elbow. Makes sense now!'

'I thought you knew what he did.'

'No, I didn't. Maybe that's why he has gone off sex.'

'What do you mean?'

'Well, if you were a dentist, the last thing you would want to see when you came home would be more teeth, wouldn't it?'

'Oh, I never thought about that.'

'You can have too much of a good thing, you know. Now tell me, what's he like as a driver?'

'Dreadful. But why do you ask?'

'I saw a sign on a car that cut me up one day. It said, "I'm a vet, that's why I drive like an animal". I remember thinking at the time, what the hell does a gynaecologist drive like then? Seems I was right!'

Mandy laughed. 'I see what you mean. Yes, he drives much too fast and cuts people up, so I suppose you could say he drives like a —'

'Hello, Roger.' Lewis came out of his office and interrupted her. 'Before we start on cross-country work, I want to consolidate your circuit training by introducing you to some other take-off and landing techniques such as the short field technique.'

'OK Lewis, let's go for it.'

'Mandy, can you book us out in Hotel-Tango please.'

'Will do, Lewis.'

CHAPTER TWENTY-EIGHT

Hotel-Tango was at the holding point for runway two-six, with checks complete.

'Now I want you to imagine you are in a farmers field,' said Lewis, 'and you've checked in the flight manual that the distance available is sufficient, considering the slope of the field, the length of the grass and the prevailing wind. Now, select one stage of flap, and we're ready to go.'

'Linton Tower, Hotel-Tango, ready for take-off.'

'Hotel-Tango cleared take-off, left-hand circuits, QFE One-Zero-One-Two, Wind calm.'

'Cleared take off, One-Zero-One-Two, Hotel-Tango.'

Roger taxied on to the runway.

'Now hold the aircraft with the brakes, apply full power, check temps and pressures, hold the elevators aft of neutral to take the weight off the nose wheel and let the brakes go,' said Lewis.

Roger put his toes on the brakes and applied full power. He pulled back slightly on the control column and let the brakes off.

'Now keep straight with the rudder as the aircraft accelerates, release the back pressure on the elevators, so we don't sink into the ground and at 55Kts rotate and keep that best angle of climb speed until we are clear of all obstacles.'

As the aircraft reached 55Kts, Roger pulled back on the control column and became airborne.

'Excellent, Roger. Well done. Now lower the nose, increase the speed to 80Kts and retract the flaps. Now fly a normal circuit until we turn base leg.'

Roger was enjoying himself. He was used to the aeroplane now and things were starting to feel natural. As he progressed downwind, he glanced over at his house. The area looked like a model village. WHAT? He was shocked to see two cars on his drive. One was Alison's but who did the other one belong to and why was Alison not at work? She had gone off as normal and not said anything was different.

She's there with Dan, thought Roger *What are they up to?*

'Wake up, Roger,' said Lewis, 'call downwind.'

Roger struggled to bring his mind back to flying the aircraft. 'Hotel-Tango, downwind.'

'Roger, Hotel-Tango. Cleared to finals, number one, runway two-six, QFE One-Zero-One-Two.'

'Clear to finals two-six, One-Zero-One-Two, Hotel-Tango.'

'OK, get the downwind checks done now so you can concentrate on the short field approach,' said Lewis.

Roger ran through the checks, trying to put Alison and Dan out of his mind.

'OK, turn base leg but reduce power more than usual, as we don't want to be too high on finals,' said Lewis. 'Now one stage flaps and trim for 80Kts. Turn finals about four hundred feet.'

'Hotel-Tango, finals.'

'Roger, Hotel-Tango. Cleared land two-six. Wind calm.'

'Cleared land two-six. Hotel-Tango.'

'Lower full flap and trim for 70Kts. Notice the flatter approach,' said Lewis, 'Now before the boundary, reduce the power slightly, raise the nose and trim for 60Kts. Now as soon as the main wheels touch, shut the throttle and brake. Easy to do on a large aerodrome, a bit more difficult in a farmers field.'

CHAPTER TWENTY-NINE

Roger and Lewis walked back into Flight Training.

'Well done Roger, although you did seem to lose your concentration a bit towards the end.' Lewis disappeared back into his office.

Roger looked over at Mandy, who was holding a phone to her ear.

'No, I've tried his mobile as well, but it seems to be switched off,' she said, 'so I can't help you, I'm afraid. OK, goodbye.'

'Problems?' asked Roger.

'Yes, that was Moldon Hospital. They've got an emergency, and they're trying to contact Dan. They say he's having a day off, but he didn't say anything to me. He went to work as normal this morning.'

'I can tell you where he is.'

'You can. How?'

'I think he's round my house with Alison.'

'What? How do you know?'

'I just flew over my house and there are two cars on the drive. One is Alison's, so I presume the other belongs to Dan. Alison went to work normally this morning as well.'

'What are those two up to, Roger?'

'I'm not sure. Lunch has turned into something else. Ring the hospital back and say they can reach him on Linton 3125. If he asks how the hospital knew he was there, then tell them to say that Mandy told them.'

'Oh, what a splendid idea, Roger. What fun!' Mandy picked the phone up and dialled. 'Hello Mary? Yes, it's Mandy. I think you can reach Dan on Linton 3125. That's correct. If he asks where you got the number from, say it was from me. OK, bye.'

Mandy turned to Roger and laughed. 'That should shock him if they phone him at your house.'

'Maybe Alison won't answer the phone. After all, she should be at work.'

'Don't you want to go home and confront them?'

'No. I can't say I'm bothered to be honest.

Alison is a pain in the arse, like her Mother. The apple didn't fall far from the tree.'

'I'm amazed at Dan, not that I'm bothered either. It hasn't been working out for some time now. Is the seat still spare for the trip to Jersey?'

'I think so. Are you going to come with me?'

'Yes, although I think Guy is going, isn't he? He really does get on my nerves. He's always having a go at me.'

'Well, he's taking Enis, so he may be a different person, you know, trying to impress her.'

'You could be right. Yes, OK, I'll definitely come with you.'

'Good, we'll have a great time. I'll confirm the seat with George if he's in the bar tonight. Are you going to join me later?'

'Yes, you bet I am. If Dan can take a day off to be with your wife, then I don't see any problem with having a drink with you.'

'Just a drink?'

'Down boy! We were lucky Mr Hamilton didn't get me the sack the other night. I'm not doing that again.'

'I'll have to find another venue. I'll give it some thought. See you in the bar later?'

'You bet.'

CHAPTER THIRTY

Roger walked into the bar. It was almost empty. Kingsley and Fidel had returned from their business trip. Kingsley had just served a customer and Fidel was standing on a chair cleaning the glass on the strange cabinet which had been built in the window between the bars.

'Pint is it, Roger?'

'Yes please, Kingsley. I hope you had a successful trip?'

'Yes, we think so,' said Kingsley, pulling Roger's pint. 'We've arranged a good deal with a brewery for real ales, lager and soft drinks, plus I've found a wholesaler nearby for supplies for my kitchen.'

'Oh good, we're all looking forward to having a proper club again, after the indignity that was Chantelle.'

Kingsley put a pint on the bar. 'There you are, Roger. Four pounds please.'

Roger put four pounds on the bar and looked around the club. He spotted Guy sitting in a corner and went over. 'Hello Guy, quiet in here today.'

'Yes, it is. That's why I thought I'd sit in the corner and finish my crossword.'

'And have you finished it?'

'Well, I'm not sure about a couple of my answers. Four across, essentially feminine, four letters ending in UNT?'

'Aunt?'

'Oh yes, Aunt. Now, why didn't I think of that? Aunt, OK so that makes four down begin with an A instead of a C. How about eleven down, found at the bottom of a budgie's cage, four letters ending IT?'

'Grit?'

'Grit! Of course. Hey, you are quite good at this Roger, you won't believe what I put.'

'Oh, I think I would, Guy.'

'OK, so try your hand at this one. Six across, overworked postman.'

'Overworked postman? OK, how many letters?'

'Loads and loads, that's why he was

overworked!'

'Oh dear, I can't believe I fell for that old one.'

Roger looked across the club at Fidel, who was now putting some strange looking objects into the glass cabinet.

'What the ??' said Roger, 'Guy, what the hell is Fidel putting in that cabinet?'

Guy looked up from his crossword. 'Oh my Lord. It's starting to look like an Ann Summers shop window.'

'This must be the cabinet of curiosities Piers told me about. He wouldn't say exactly what it was, and I think I see why now.'

'You don't think they are going to sell those, do you?'

'I've no idea. I would imagine it's probably a collection they've accumulated, perhaps during the time they've been together. I do hope they've washed them all properly.'

CHAPTER THIRTY-ONE

Roger rushed over to George as soon as he appeared through the club door.

'George is that last seat still vacant on the Jersey trip?'

'Yes. Has Mandy decided to join us?'

'Indeed she has.'

'OK, so we have a full house. Steve will be in later, then we can order some duty-free from the bo—,' George caught sight of the cabinet, 'what on earth is that?'

'It's Kingsley and Fiddles' Cabinet of Curiosities.'

George was lost for words. 'I think I need a pint and a sit-down.'

'Go and sit with Guy in the corner, and I'll get a round in.'

'Make mine a G and T, please.'

'Oh hello Mandy, I didn't see you sneak in. You're definitely booked in for the Jersey trip. Kingsley, three pints and a G and T please.'

'What is in that cabinet on the wall over there?' asked Mandy, screwing her eyes up. 'Oh, are they what I think they are?'

'Yes, sex toys I think you would call them.'

'Oh yes,' said Mandy, getting quite excited.

'Do you fancy any of them?'

'I'd love that big red one, please!'

'What big red one?' said Roger, 'Oh, you idiot, that's the bloody fire extinguisher.'

'Oh, what a shame!'

'Well, I suppose you have been rather spoilt recently. Here, take your G and T, and George's pint. We're sitting in the corner with Guy.'

Roger paid Kingsley and carried the remaining two pints across to the table.

'Are we going to have to sit here and look at the Cabinet of Curiosities every time we come in here for a drink?' asked George.

'Well we could complain to Kingsley and Fiddle about it, but I doubt it would have much effect. Piers told me they take it everywhere they go. They use it as a sort of centrepiece.'

'I suppose we'll get used to it. Ah, here comes Steve. Get your duty-free orders ready,' said George, 'Sorry Steve, Roger just got a round in, so you'll have to buy your own beer.'

Steve pulled a face but went to the bar.

'Does everybody know what they want?'

Everybody nodded. 'Is there a price list, so we can see what's on offer and how much things cost?' asked Roger.

'We can ask.'

Steve returned from the bar with a pint, sat down and got out a notebook and pen. He looked around. 'OK, who wants what?'

'Have you got a price list?' asked George, 'people are wondering what's on offer and at what price.'

'No, they said they don't do one, but they do what you find on aircraft and in duty-free shops. Spirits, fags and perfume.'

'OK,' said Roger, 'put me down for a bottle of Glenfiddich.'

'I'll have the same, and a bottle of Smirnoff vodka for Enis,' said Guy.

'I'd like a bottle of Gordon's gin please,' said Mandy.

'I'll take a bottle of Jim Beam,' said George, 'and can you find me a nice Ladies watch? The wife's just broken hers.'

'OK, all noted. I'll see what I can do in the morning.'

'Not ordering any perfume, Mandy?' asked Guy, 'Isn't perfume what a woman put behind her ears to make herself attractive to a man?'

'Yes, of course it is.'

'No Mandy, it's her ankles,' said Guy, 'Now, I thought you of all people would have known that!'

CHAPTER THIRTY-TWO

'Oh no,' said Roger, 'it's Vic from Hell
and his mates.'

They all looked up and Vic and several
friends had entered the club. They all
stopped in their tracks to stare at the cabinet
of curiosities. It became obvious from the
look on their faces most of them
disapproved. Led by Vic, they walked over
to the bar and Kingsley came to serve them.

'Good evening gentlemen, what can I get
you?'

'I want to see the landlord.'

'I am the landlord.'

'No not you, I ain't even seen you before.
The other one.'

'Oh Fidel, you mean. I'll call him.' He
went to the cellar door, 'Fidel, someone to

see you.'

After a few moments, Fidel appeared.
'Yes?'

'No not him. I ain't seen him before
either. The landlord, the posh bloke, I saw
him yesterday.'

'Oh Piers, you mean. He's merely a
barman. We are the landlords.'

'Well it's him I want to see, that Piers. He
threatened to throw me out yesterday
because I used the word cock, and yet we
come in here today and there's a cabinet full
of cocks on the wall. What's going on?'

'Piers was quite correct in admonishing
you for swearing, it's something we don't
allow in the bar. The cabinet of curiosities
on the wall is our collection of toys we have
accumulated since Fidel and I have been
together. Now, what would you like to
drink?'

Vic looked at his friends and they all
nodded. He turned back to Kingsley. 'Four
pints of bitter please.'

Kingsley pulled four pints and put them
on the bar. 'Sixteen pounds please.'

Vic put sixteen pounds on the bar. Just
then all the lights went out. Luckily it wasn't
quite dark outside.

'Power cut,' said Fidel, 'I've got some candles in the cellar.'

He went into the cellar and returned a few moments later with a tray containing a box of candles, some saucers and a box of matches. He went round each table, lighting a candle and sticking it on a saucer.

'Well that entertainment went a bit flat,' said George, 'I thought Vic was going to kick off more than that.'

'Alcohol trumps all other considerations, I think,' said Roger, 'I wonder what the power problem is?'

'It's probably deliberate,' said Mandy, 'done to save us all from Guy's disco.'

George stood up and walked to the window. 'There are lights in the tower and offices, but they must have an emergency generator.'

Vic sat fiddling with his candle, breaking bits of wax off from where it had run down the side, then melting the pieces in the flame at the top. Fidel lent on the bar, watching him with growing annoyance until he could contain it no longer. He straightened up, walked round to Vic's table and snatched the candle away from him.

'We don't do that sort of thing in here.'

Vic looked up at him. 'No? But you seem to do a lot of things that are perverted.'

'Perverted? Perverted?' wailed Fidel, 'Oh that's the worst possible thing you could have said.'

'Perverted? Who's perverted?' boomed Kingsley from the kitchen door.

'You two are,' said Vic. 'Look at that cabinet.'

Kingsley came out into the bar and joined Fidel. 'Right, out now, and take your friends with you. Your memberships are all cancelled. Don't come in here again or I'll call the police.'

'What about refunding our ten-pound memberships?' protested Vic.

'So sue us,' said Kingsley, 'Unfortunately, you paid your money to someone else, not to us. Sue them, if you can find them. Now bugger off, before I call the police now.'

Vic and his three friends reluctantly stood up, finished their drinks and left.

Kingsley and Fidel followed them outside, to make sure they left the premises. They returned to a round of applause.

'Thankfully, we won't have to see that lot any more,' said Roger, just as the lights came back on again.

'Oh no,' said Mandy, 'Bloody lights. That means Guy's disco is back on again.'

CHAPTER THIRTY-THREE

'Who fancies another drink?' asked George.

Everybody nodded, so George got up and went to the bar. 'Can I have four pints and a G and T please Kingsley?'

'Certainly George,' replied Kingsley.

'So when are you starting the food and what's on the menu?'

'Well I've not finalised the menu yet but it will be things like peppered steak, Moules marineres, home-cooked pies, cheesy chips at night and a range of salads at lunchtime.'

'Luckily I won't be in here at lunchtime but the evening menu sounds great.'

'Well as soon as I've finalised it, I'll give you your own copy, George. If there's anything else you fancy or think would be popular, just let me know. There's no point in cooking things that nobody wants.'

'I'll give it some thought, Kingsley.'

'That would be really helpful, George. Now four pints and a G and T, that's twenty-one pounds please. Here's a tray to carry them back on.'

George paid Kingsley, picked up the tray and returned to the table, only to find an argument going on.

'Guy was in the Fleawick supermarket earlier, and he thought he saw his nickname on a loaf of bread,' said Mandy, 'but when he got closer, he realised that it just said thick cut,'

'Well, that's very ladylike.'

'Well I'm fed up with your constant jokes about me, Guy. What's the difference between your jokes and your penis?'

'My jokes are quite short?'

'No! Nobody laughs at your bloody jokes, Guy.'

'Whoa, whoa, people' said George, putting the tray down on the table, 'Look, we're all off on a lovely trip to Jersey tomorrow to have fun. Can't we all grow up and get along?'

'I'm just sick of his constant jibes at me.'

124

'Guy, come on, give it a rest,' said Roger.

Guy got up. 'Time for my disco, I think,' and he disappeared off to his stage.

'So what time are we meeting here tomorrow morning, George,' asked Roger.

'Nine o'clock, as usual. Steve, presumably you'll be here a bit earlier to sort the duty-free out?'

'Yes, I'll have it all done by nine.'

'OK, I'll see you all at nine.'

Over on the stage, Guy commenced his disco.

'Good evening, Ladies and Gentlemen. Welcome to the Cloud Nine disco with your host, Prince Charles.'

'I'll start tonight as always by reading today's main stories from your local rag, the Linton, Fleawick and Moldon Evening Gazette.'

'The main story tonight is that Donald Campbell's body has been found at last. Apparently it came out of a tap in Huddersfield.'

'Oxford University has released the results of research into why women are more intelligent than men. Yes, it's because women don't marry men just because they have large breasts.'

'And the Nuclear Reprocessing plant at Sellafield admitted today that safety records had been tampered with. A spokesman said it was nothing to worry about as the number of times this had happened could be counted on the fingers of one foot. Sellafield is of course twined with Molden, for similar orthopaedic reasons.'

'So I'll start tonight's session with Broadripple Is Burning by Margot and The Nuclear So and Sos.'

'Time to go?' asked Roger.

'Yes,' said Mandy.

'I'll see you to your car.'

They left the club and went into the car park. Darkness had descended.

'I see you've parked in the far corner again,' said Roger, 'any particular reason for that?'

'Well, sometimes a nice chap sees me to my car. Last time, he had a bulky object in his trousers. This time I thought I'd find out what it was.'

CHAPTER THIRTY-FOUR

Roger and Alison were eating breakfast. Alison was burying her head in the newspaper.

'So did the hospital manage to contact Dan?'

Alison grunted.

'Sorry, I didn't catch that?'

'Yes, they did.'

'Oh good. Some sort of emergency, I believe?'

Alison grunted again.

'Fortunate that someone knew his whereabouts then.'

'Yes, wasn't it? How did Mandy know where to find Dan? Has she paid someone to follow him?'

'No, she hasn't.'

'Well, how did she know then?'

'I told her.'

'You? You told her? How the hell did you know?'

'The eye in the sky. I was doing circuits, happened to glance down and saw two cars on the drive. One was yours, so it didn't take much to guess who the other one belonged to.'

Alison shook her head in disbelief. 'There's no bloody hiding place.'

'When I got back to the club, Mandy said the hospital was desperate to find Dan. I gave her our number, and she passed it on.'

Alison put her head in her hands.

'So what exactly was he doing here, may I ask?'

Alison said nothing. Roger could see her squirming, and he was thoroughly enjoying every minute of it.

'Professional visit perhaps? Or moonlighting for Gynorod?'

'Shut up, Roger.'

'Well, I thought he might have taken a look down there to see what the blockage was. You two seem to get on so well that I'm sure the furry cup will come into play at some point.'

'Don't be such a hypocrite, Roger. Just think what you've been doing to Mandy at every opportunity. I expect you'll be seeing her later today.'

'I will. We're going on a day trip to Jersey together. But the poor girl wasn't going to come with me until she found out what you two were up to yesterday. That made her mind up.'

'I'm sure you'll have a lovely day.'

'I'm sure we will. Mandy enjoys life rather than looking for things to moan about as you do.'

'Oh shut up Roger, you are bloody impossible. I'm going to work.'

'Are you sure about that or are you meeting Dan?'

Alison went out the door and slammed it behind her. BANG!

CHAPTER THIRTY-FIVE

Roger walked into Flight Training reception. 'Morning all.'

'Hello Roger, we're all here then except Mandy,' said George, 'Let's go into the briefing area and plan the flight.'

'Oh, I thought Mandy would be here already, she's always such an early bird.'

'Up with the early morning cock, I suppose,' said Guy.

'Guy, please not to be so rude about Mandy,' said Enis.

'Thank you, Enis, do try to keep him in order today, please.'

'OK, Roger, will do.'

George and Roger went off into the briefing area.

'Now you remember the Gen Decs and

flight plan from last time? Well, we've had to do those already. Steve has taken the Gen Decs to Customs to get them stamped as that's the only way the bond will release the duty-free. He'll drop off the flight plan while he's in the tower and then pick up the duty-free on the way back.'

'OK.'

'Now let's look at the weather. We've got a ridge of high pressure over southern England and the channel which is giving us the nice weather at the moment but that is declining as a cold front moves across from the west.'

'I don't think that will worry us today,' said Roger, 'so it looks like a nice flight there and back.'

'OK, so we are nearly done but as we're going to the Channel Isles,' George continued, 'we need to visit Special Branch. Let's rejoin the others.'

They walked back into reception just as an ashen-faced Mandy walked through the front door.

'Hello Mandy, are you alright?' asked Roger, 'you look terrible. Why are you late?'

'Oh I'm sorry, I had a bang in the car on the way here.'

'Bloody hell,' said Guy, 'can't you control your sexual urges? Keeping us all waiting.'

'Not that sort of bang, you blithering idiot, I mean I had an accident in the car, I've bent the wing on our gatepost.'

'How did you do that?' asked Roger.

'I was in a state because Dan got a call from Alison. She let him know we were off to Jersey together today. He didn't want me to go, and we had an argument. I got in the car and fled but I caught the gatepost on the way out. I had to stop in a lay-by for a while to recover.'

Roger put his arm around her. 'Come here. I'm sorry, it's my fault. I let it slip but it never occurred to me she would tip Dan off. She is so vindictive.'

'Well, Dan was still annoyed about being caught out yesterday, so that didn't help.'

'Ah, here's Steve now,' said George, 'so we can all go to Special Branch together.'

They all left reception and made their way over to the Special Branch office. As they passed Mandy's car, they stopped to assess the damage.

'It's not that bad,' said Roger, 'Just two big bumps and a large gash.'

'What, Mandy or the car?' asked Guy.

'Guy, you are being rude again,' said Enis, 'cannot you see Mandy is very upset?'

They walked into the Special Branch office. 'Oh, you two again,' said the chap behind the counter, 'Jernsey again, is it? Here get your passengers to fill out these forms.'

'Jersey today,' said George, picking up the forms and handing them out, 'fill these in, and we'll be on our way.'

'Oh, these look complicated,' said Mandy, looking at the forms, 'Pity Dan's not here!'

'Why?' asked Roger.

'Because he's an expert at checking boxes.'

CHAPTER THIRTY-SIX

The six left the Special Branch office and walked over to the aircraft.

'They were quite human, just like I told you, weren't they?' said George to Roger.

'Yes, everyone seems so nice and friendly.'

'Well they have a job to do, just like customs, but they realise most people are genuine, and they are the people they are there to protect.'

'So what do they do with the information they collect from us?'

'Well, Special Branch is the political police. All those details go off to MI5, when and where we went, and when we came back. I'm sure they check our backgrounds, whether we have any sympathy towards the IRA or indeed any relatives or friends that are known to them.'

'What about Customs?'

'Much the same, I suppose. Do we keep going to drug hot spots or are any of our passengers known drug users or dealers.'

'Makes sense.'

'Yes, it does. It can go wrong though. We came back from Amsterdam once and Customs turned us over. May have been random or maybe one of our passengers had previous. They even wanted to open someone's camera, but we persuaded them not to ruin his pictures. The drugs dog had already sniffed it. Pointless.'

They reached the aircraft, loaded the duty-free into the front hold and climbed aboard. George and Steve into the pilots' seats and Roger, Mandy, Guy and Enis facing each other in the rear club-style seating.

George started the engine and called the tower. 'Linton Tower, Golf-Zulu-Oscar-Oscar-November, request taxi for departure to Jersey.'

'Roger Oscar-November. Cleared taxi to the holding point runway two-six, QNH One-Zero-One-Five.'

'Cleared taxi holding point two-six, QNH

One-Zero-One-Five. Oscar-November.'

George opened the throttle and began taxiing toward the holding point.

'Enis, have you ever been in a light aircraft before?' asked Roger.

'No. It is my first time. There is not much room for legs, is there?'

'Well Mandy is OK because she's used to putting them behind her ears,' said Guy.

Mandy had had enough. She lifted her heel off the floor and thrust it between Guy's legs. Guy went very quiet.

'Linton Tower, Oscar-November ready for take-off.'

'Roger Oscar-November. Cleared take-off runway two-six, QNH One-Zero-One-Five, wind 250 15 knots.'

'Cleared take-off two-six, One-Zero-One-Five, Oscar-November.'

George taxied on to the runway and opened the throttle. Soon they were airborne.

'Oscar-November, airborne at three-five. Call London Information on One-Two-Four-Decimal-Six.'

'London Information One-Two-Four-Decimal-Six. Oscar-November. Bye.'

CHAPTER THIRTY-SEVEN

'Oh look, there are The Needles,' said Mandy as the aircraft flew just to the west of the Isle of Wight.

'What are needles?' asked Enis.

'Look down there, those chalk pillars sticking out of the sea are called The Needles.'

'Oh, and what is the red and white thing at the end?'

'That's a lighthouse with a helicopter landing pad on top.'

'Not much more to see now until we reach Cap de la Hague,' said George.

Oscar-November flew on at three thousand feet over the channel, passing over several ships in one of the busiest shipping lanes in the world.

'Jersey Zone, Golf-Zulu-Oscar-Oscar-November inbound to you from Linton, three thousand feet on One-Zero-One-Eight,' said Steve.

'Roger Oscar-November, squawk 3621 with IDENT, call crossing Fifty North.'

'Squawk 3621, call crossing Fifty North. Oscar-November.'

Steve dialled 3621 into the transponder and pressed INDENT. He checked the distance to the Jersey VOR, waiting for it to read forty five nautical miles, which would indicate the latitude of fifty degrees north of the equator.

'Jersey Zone, Oscar-November crossing Fifty North.'

'Roger Oscar-November, identified at Fifty North. Continue via the Cap to Jersey runway two-seven. Call Jersey Approach One-Two-Zero-Decimal-Three.'

'Via the Cap for two-seven, Approach One-Two-Zero-Decimal-Three, Bye.'

'Look there is Cap de la Hague off our port wing,' said George, 'and that industrial site is a nuclear fuel reprocessing plant.'

'And off our starboard wing is Alderney,' said Steve, 'the third largest of the Channel Isles.'

'You can just see Jersey in the distance,' said George.

'Jersey Approach, Oscar-November passing the Cap, three thousand feet on One-Zero-One-Eight,' said Steve.

'Roger Oscar-November. Traffic information, in your twelve o'clock, right to left is a Fokker F27, one thousand feet above.'

'Thanks, we have the Fokker in sight.'

'Roger Oscar-November. Continue at three thousand feet on One-Zero-One-Eight.'

'Continue. Oscar-November.'

Oscar-November flew on at three thousand feet and from that altitude, all the islands were visible.

'Oscar-November, do you have the airfield in sight?'

'Oscar November, affirmative.'

'Oscar-November, further descent at your discretion, call the tower on One-One-Nine-Decimal-Four-Five.'

'Call Tower on One-One-Nine-Decimal-Four-Five, Oscar-November.'

Steve switched to the other radio. 'Jersey Tower, Oscar November passing two thousand feet for runway two-seven.'

'Roger Oscar-November, you're cleared to land runway two-seven, QFE One-Zero-Zero-Nine, wind 230 degrees at 10Kts.'

'Cleared land two-seven, One-Zero-Zero-Nine. Oscar-November.'

George reduced the power and turned towards the airport. At one thousand feet, he lowered the undercarriage.

Landing on the numbers, he selected the first taxiway and taxied to park in the grass area with the other light aircraft.

CHAPTER THIRTY-EIGHT

After clearing all the airport formalities, the six emerged into the terminal building.

'We need to hire a car for the day,' said George, 'I'll go to one of the desks and get a small minibus. Then lunch!'

George returned a few minutes later rattling some keys. 'Minibus, in the car park. Let's find it.'

They walked around the car park and eventually found the minibus.

'All aboard. We're a bit early for lunch, so I'll take you to the Lobster Pot via the pretty route.'

He turned right out of the airport and headed down to Red Houses. Turning right again he pointed to a row of small trees in front of some houses.

'There used to be a row of enormous trees here but Michael Fish's hurricane in 1987 flattened the lot of them, and they fell onto those houses. We were here a week later and saw the devastation.'

He turned right in La Moye and headed down to Five Mile Beach.

As they drove along, Guy spotted some nudists. 'Is this a nudist beach, George?'

'Not officially, but I don't think anyone minds.'

Guy let the window down for a better view. 'Good Lord, look at the knockers on that one!'

Enis dug him in the ribs. 'Behave Guy.'

'If it's knockers that you're into Guy, you should have come with us to the beach in Biarritz, France,' said George, 'it had more tits than Bill Oddie's garden!'

They continued along Five Mile Beach. Near the top end, George slowed down and pointed to a field.

'It was in that field that I first made love.'

'Too much information,' said Mandy.

'Well I only mention it,' George continued, 'because her mother came by and caught us at it!'

'Oh no,' said Mandy, 'how awful, what

on earth did she say?'

'Baa.'

Every one laughed. 'Oh you had us going there,' said Mandy.

George turned off through L'Etacq to the Lobster Pot and parked in the car park. 'Anyone that doesn't like seafood or fillet steak can stay on the bloody bus!'

They walked into the restaurant. A waiter came to greet them, 'A table for six? Come this way.'

That's an improvement on the restaurant in Le Touquet thought Roger.

They all sat at the table perusing the menu.

'Wow, I've never seen so much seafood on a menu,' said Roger.

'I'm sure they'll wipe it off if you ask,' said Guy.

'Crabs, lobsters, langoustines, plaice, bouillabaisse, wow brilliant,' continued Roger, 'I love all that.'

'Lobster Bisque with brandy and cream,' said George, 'followed by a fillet steak, and loads of profiteroles.'

'Steak for me,' said Enis.

'And for me,' said Guy.

'I fancy the plaice,' said Mandy.

'I'd have thought you would have gone for the Coq au vin, Mandy,' said Guy, 'even though we've got a minibus.'

Mandy swung her foot under the table but just failed to connect with Guy's nether regions.

CHAPTER THIRTY-NINE

'Wow, I can hardly walk,' said Mandy as they all staggered out of the Lobster Pot.

'I think that is the best meal I've ever had,' said Roger.

They all climbed back into the minibus.

'Where do you want to go now?' asked George.

'Can we go to the shops?' asked Mandy, 'I hear jewellery is cheap in Jersey.'

'Oh yes please,' agreed Enis.

'Well if there are no objections then, we'll head to St Helier.'

Twenty minutes later, George found a parking space near the centre of St Helier.

'Lots of shops to choose from, girls' said Steve, 'don't go mad.'

Mandy and Enis shot off and went to look

in the nearest jeweller's window. The boys followed at a distance.

'Oh that necklace is lovely and a lot cheaper than home,' said Mandy.

'That bracelet is cheap as well,' said Enis, 'let's go inside and have closer look. Come on Guy.'

The girls went into the shop, closely followed by the boys.

George and Steve stood at the back of the shop and watched as jewellery spread across the counter, as the girls tried to make up their minds what to purchase.

'If we get out of here before closing time, I'll be very surprised,' yawned George, 'what is it about women and shopping?'

Eventually, purchase decisions were made, and they were ready to leave.

As they all came out of the shop, it was apparent something had changed. The sun had disappeared and there was a moist chill in the air.

George looked up at the sky, 'Oh no, must be sea fog!'

'What's that?' asked Roger.

'When an area of warm moist air gets blown over a cold sea, the sea can cool the air to below its dew point and form fog. It's a coastal phenomenon.'

'So is that a problem?'

'Yes. Fog can completely cover an island like Jersey and shut the airport. But there was nothing on the forecast this morning. I'll ring Jersey Met and see what's happening.'

George went off to a quiet corner and got on his mobile.

'What's all this mean?' asked Mandy.

'We may be stuck here until it clears,' said Steve.

'What for an hour, two hours?'

'We'll find out when George gets off his phone.'

George returned with a grim face. 'Bad news, I'm afraid. Visibility at the airport is down below a hundred metres. Incoming flights are already turning back. They're not expecting clearance until the morning when the cold front comes through. We're stuck.'

'Why nothing on the forecast?' asked Roger.

'It was expected to go further west. The wind has changed slightly and brought it here.'

'So what do we do?' asked Mandy.

'Find a hotel. Look on the bright side, we get to eat another nice meal, and we can go on the piss in St Helier! Lots of nice bars and restaurants.'

Mandy and Roger looked at each other and thought *Oh no. This won't go down well with our spouses. They'll never believe we didn't arrange it.*

CHAPTER FORTY

'If we walk up the road a bit there's a tourist information booth,' said Steve, 'they can tell us which hotels have vacancies.'

They continued up the road to the booth. 'What do we want people? Two doubles and a twin room, bed and breakfast? Yes?'

They all agreed. Steve paid a deposit and took some tickets to give to the hotel.

'It's not far. It's got a restaurant and a bar, so we won't need to go out again if we don't want to.'

'That was very easy,' said Mandy, 'I thought we would have trouble finding somewhere at such short notice.'

'Not at this time of year,' said George, 'If you came in August when the Battle of Flowers is on, or in September when the

149

International Air Display is on, then it would be a completely different story.'

They reached the hotel, looked at the rooms and decided to accept.

'I'm not sure about you lot,' said George, 'but I could murder a pint. This place seems very pleasant so shall we adjourn to the bar?'

Roger looked at Mandy. 'We'll catch you all up. We need to ring our other halves and let them know we won't be back tonight. It's not going to be an easy conversation for either of us!'

Later, they all sat in the bar together. Mandy and Enis spotted some cream cake in a cabinet at the bar and disappeared off to drool.

'I think you should do a risk assessment in your room Guy,' said Roger, 'check where the radiators are and any other solid objects. You don't want another accident.'

'Ha bloody ha, Roger,' said Guy, 'Look, I'll make a small wager with you that I'll have more sex than you tonight!'

'Don't think so, mate, Mandy is in top form, so you're on. Ten pounds, OK?'

'Twenty.'

'OK, twenty. But we can't let the girls

know what's going on, they wouldn't like it. How can we keep it to ourselves?'

'We'll settle it at breakfast in the morning. We'll order a slice of toast for every time we had sex. How about that?'

'Sounds good to me, they'll have no idea what we're at.'

In the morning, the six met for breakfast at eight o'clock. They sat around a circular table. There was lots of yawning.

'Did everybody sleep alright?' asked George.

Guy and Enis giggled. 'Yes thank you.'

Roger and Mandy just smiled.

'Alright, alright, it was a bloody silly question,' said George, 'Ah, here comes the waiter. Full English for me please.'

'Same for me,' said Steve.

'I'll take the kippers,' said Mandy.

'Can I have porridge please?' asked Enis.

'Full English for me please, and three slices of toast,' said Roger with a smile. He looked triumphantly at Guy.

'Full English for me as well and four slices of toast,' said Guy, 'Oh, and can you make one of the slices brown please.'

CHAPTER FORTY-ONE

George drove the minibus up the airport approach road. 'Well at least the fog has gone but this cold front looks pretty active. It could be a very bumpy ride home.'

'I hope you've got a good bra on Mandy,' said Guy, 'otherwise it could get a bit dangerous in the back!'

'It'll definitely be dangerous in the back if you don't shut up,' said Mandy, 'because my foot will find your bollocks again.' Guy winced as he remembered the flight over.

'Guy, why are you always so nasty to Mandy,' asked Enis, 'When you help me out in the bar, I think Guy is nice man. Now I'm not sure.'

They parked the minibus in the car park and made their way into the terminal.

'Steve and I will go up to the Met Office and check on the weather. Roger, you should come as well. They've got weather radar, so you can actually see the nasty areas rather than just guess.'

'Right, that sounds interesting,' said Roger.

They climbed the stairs in what was the original terminal building for Jersey airport, the same stairs as the Nazis must have used when they landed at the airport in June 1940.

They filed a flight plan and checked the weather in the Met Office. A cold front lay from Jersey to the centre of the UK.

'Can we have a look at your weather radar please?' asked George.

'Of course, do come in,' said the forecaster.

The weather radar showed the actual situation in greater detail. A line of heavy showers and the odd thunderstorm stretched between Jersey and Central England.

'We'll just have to dodge them as best we can,' said George, 'Once the front moves on, we'll be behind them.'

They made their way back to the others

and then to the aircraft.

Once airborne, Steve climbed the aircraft to two thousand feet until they were clear of the Jersey Zone and had established contact with Southampton for further climb.

The aircraft was level at three thousand feet, flying in and out of clouds when darkness suddenly descended. A giant hand seemed to pick them up and lift them rapidly to nearly four thousand feet. As Steve pushed forward on the control column to descend back towards three thousand feet, the giant hand decided to drop them and pelt them with hailstones. The noise from the stones became intense. In the back, both the girls screamed. The aircraft began to descend and Steve had to pull back on the control column to maintain the desired level.

'I've had enough of this,' said Steve and pressed the PTT button. 'Southampton Approach, Oscar-November. We've hit a bad patch of weather, can you give us vectors to clear it please?'

'Oscar-November, roger. Turn left thirty degrees and you should be out of it in two miles.'

'Thirty degrees left, thanks, Oscar-November.'

Steve banked the aircraft to the left, turning onto a northerly heading. The hail stopped and about a minute later they popped out of the cloud into brilliant sunshine. Everyone breathed a sigh of relief.

'Oh that was horrible,' said Mandy, 'I thought I was going to die.'

'That was a cumulonimbus cloud,' explained George, 'the sort thunderstorms are made of. Huge updraughts and downdraught's.'

'Oscar-November, Southampton Approach, if you resume your original heading now, you'll be in the clear all the way to Linton.'

'Resuming original heading and thank you for your help. Oscar-November.'

The rest of the flight was sunny and uneventful. Steve landed on the numbers back at Linton and taxied back to the club. The occupants disembarked.

'I'm glad that's over,' said Mandy, 'That was really frightening for a while.'

'I thought it was educational,' said Roger, 'getting experience like that while I'm learning to fly. Thanks, George, thanks, Steve.'

They unloaded the duty-free from the

front hold and made their way into the club.

George and Steve worked out the cost of the flight and hotel, Steve the individual costs of the duty-free.

'Anyone fancy a drink?' asked George.

They all declined the offer.

Roger looked at Mandy. 'What sort of reception do you think we'll get at home?'

Mandy winced. 'Not good Roger, not good. To make it worse, I've got a bent car and gatepost to worry about.'

CHAPTER FORTY-TWO

Roger and Alison were eating breakfast.
You could have cut the air with a knife.

Roger had spoken to Alison on the phone
to let her know he was stuck in Jersey.
Alison hadn't believed him and accused him
of just wanting a dirty weekend away with
his Floozie.

Alison wasn't at home when Roger got
back from Jersey. In fact, she hadn't got
home much before midnight. Roger, who
hadn't slept much the night before, had
fallen asleep in the spare bedroom, where he
was now confined to at night, at Alison's
pleasure. He had heard her come in but
didn't feel up to having a blazing argument
at that time of night, so he had gone back to
sleep. Since they had been up this morning,

neither had uttered a word.

Roger broke the silence. 'Where were you last night, Alison? It was nearly midnight when you got in.'

Roger probably wasn't expecting much of a reply, but he was totally unprepared for Alison's response. She picked up a plate and threw it at him. It hit him on the forehead and broke, before smashing on to the floor.

'I can't believe you have the bloody cheek to ask me that, Roger,' shouted Alison, 'You take your Floozie away for a dirty weekend and then you have the temerity to ask me where I was?'.

She picked up another plate and threw it at Roger. He managed to duck this time.

A trickle of blood ran down his face. 'You're right,' he said, wiping it from his cheek with his hand, 'I have got a bloody cheek. You've cut me.'

'Good! You deserve it.'

'I explained to you we were fogged in. It was unavoidable, even the commercial aircraft weren't flying.'

'Yes, I know. Your Floozie told Dan the same.'

'Well, of course, she did. It was what

happened.'

'So where did you stay the night?'

'In a hotel of course.'

'Separate rooms?'

'There were six of us. Of course, we had separate rooms.'

'Don't be facetious Roger, you know exactly what I mean. Did you sleep with her?'

Roger was stuck. They hadn't slept much, but they probably had slept at the same time, so he couldn't wiggle out of it on a technicality. Should he be honest and admit it?

'Your silence is an admission of guilt,' said Alison.

'Never mind about me,' said Roger, holding a tissue to his injury, 'I asked you where you were until midnight last night and all I got was a hole in the head for an answer.'

'I was with Dan. His wife was having a dirty weekend away with you and he needed support.'

'It was obvious you would be with the Eunuch. But I asked you where you were.'

This seemed to upset Alison and another plate flew in Roger's direction. He didn't quite duck quick enough, and this one caught his ear.

'Don't call him that. Dan is a lovely man, worth ten of you any day.'

'Wow, you have got it bad,' said Roger, moving the tissue to mop the blood now coming from his ear, 'such passion. What have you two been up to?'

Alison went quiet for a moment. 'We've become very fond of each other. We were both devastated by our spouse's betrayals. We found solace in being together.'

'And when did you have sex?' asked Roger, 'Yesterday?'

Alison looked at Roger. 'Yes, it was yesterday. And it wasn't just because we knew you and Mandy had been at it like rabbits. It felt the natural thing to do.'

'And the Eunuch actually managed it, did he?'

Another plate whizzed its way past Roger's ear. 'Don't call him that. Yes, he did, and it was lovely. He has a good knowledge of a woman's anatomy, as you would expect, considering the job he does. And he was much better than you ever were.'

'You've still not told me where you were until midnight.'

Alison looked embarrassed. 'We were at the hospital. Dan's got a consulting room there.'

'Oh I see, and that's where you decided to play doctors and nurses I suppose. Look, he may be all lovee-dovee now, but what's he going to be like when he meets your Mother and reality sets in?'

Alison reached for another plate but then thought better of it. 'Make sure you clear all the mess up before you go and see your Floozie, Roger. I'm going to work.'

At that, Alison turned on her heel and slammed the door behind her. BANG!

More to the point thought Roger, *I'd better get my face cleaned up.*

CHAPTER FORTY-THREE

Roger walked into Flight Training reception.

Mandy was behind the counter.

'Hello Rog—, oh what on earth has happened to your face?'

'Alison happened to it, she threw plates at it. Our kitchen looked like the aftermath of a Greek wedding.'

'Oh no, that's awful. What started it off?'

'Me asking her where she was until nearly midnight.'

'I guess she was with Dan, as he didn't get back until about the same time.'

'She was, she admitted it. Did you know they've been having sex in Dan's consulting room at the hospital?'

'No, I didn't. She actually told you that?'

'Yes, she did and apparently he's much better at it than I am, all down to his professional knowledge of a woman's body.'

Mandy snorted. 'Can't say I ever noticed. Well, they seem to have hit it off, just like we have, so good luck to them I say.'

'You don't mind?'

'Mind? Why should I mind? I told you our relationship hadn't been working out for quite a while. I'm much happier being with you. Are you saying you mind?'

'Well, she is my wife.'

'Yes, and I'm Dan's wife but that hasn't stopped you, has it? Don't be a hypocrite Roger. You tell me you and Alison don't get along, in fact, you never have a good word to say about her. If she has found someone that makes her happy, then you should be pleased.'

'Yes, I suppose you're right. It's a sensible resolution to all our problems.'

'It is. And at least we don't have to pretend any more. Everyone knows what everyone else is doing.'

'You are quite the philosopher as well as being beautiful, aren't you?' said Roger, leaning across the counter and giving Mandy a kiss.

'Don't molest the staff please Roger,' said Lewis as he emerged from his office. 'Oh, your face. Are you OK to fly?'

'Yes, I'm fine Lewis. Just some domestic injuries.'

'OK if you're sure, Roger. We'll start cross-country flying today, so we need to plan a flight. Let's go into the briefing area, and check if the weather is suitable for cross-country flying.'

They went round to the briefing area. 'Now looking at the forecast, we have a high-pressure area moving in,' said Lewis, 'Cloud base is few at four thousand feet and the visibility is fifteen kilometres. That sounds fine for a flight at three thousand feet where we will be navigating purely from ground features. Do you agree?'

'Yes, makes sense.'

'I propose we fly a triangular course from Linton to these two disused airfields and back. Make a note of the three thousand feet wind which is Zero-Eight-Zero degrees at fifteen knots, that will be pushing us off course. OK?'

'Yes, fine.'

'Now from your knowledge of navigation so far, draw the tracks on your map, choose which way you want to go and work out your headings to allow for the wind and for a 90Kt airspeed.'

Roger sat down and drew the tracks on his map with his chinagraph pencil. He worked out his headings, ground speeds and timings using his CRP-1 flight computer. He transferred the details on his flight log, and then timed and marked off some interesting waypoints on the map, so he could check his progress along the route.

'I think I'm all done,' said Roger.

'OK,' said Lewis, 'let's put your flight plan to the test.'

They walked back through reception. 'Can you book us out in Hotel-Tango please Mandy.'

'Will do Lewis,' said Mandy, 'good luck Roger.'

CHAPTER FORTY-FOUR

Roger and Lewis were airborne in Hotel-Tango.

'Continue the climb straight ahead to two thousand feet and do a climbing turn to three thousand feet back overhead Linton,' said Lewis, 'we'll start your flight plan at cruising speed, dead overhead the airfield and on the correct heading.'

Roger continued the climb to three thousand feet and set the aircraft up for the cruise. As he approached the airfield, he checked and aligned the direction indicator closely with the compass.

'That's good, Roger. Accurate flying is essential in cross-country navigation. OK, so we are overhead the field, note the time and start the stopwatch.'

166

'Overhead at time one-two, stopwatch started,' said Roger.

'Now the first thing to do is to check we haven't messed up our calculations by looking for an early ground feature to confirm we are going in the right direction. What's your first ground feature?'

Oh! It's Moldon Hospital, thought Roger. He looked down and there it was. The car park was full, but he was too high to see if Alison's car was there. He began to think about Dan's consul--

'Wake up, Roger!' interrupted Lewis.

'Sorry Lewis, it's Moldon Hospital and it's just below the left-wing, as expected.'

'OK, so what is our next checkpoint?'

'A motorway junction with a river running underneath, due in five minutes.'

'OK, so put the map down and concentrate on keeping an accurate heading.'

Roger tried to concentrate on the flying but his mind kept creeping back to Moldon Hospital.

'Wake up, Roger!' said Lewis again, 'what is the matter with you? Your heading is wandering and you've almost missed your next checkpoint.'

'Oh dear, it's due in 30 seconds,' said
Roger, peering out of the front windscreen,
'but I can't see it.'

'Could be because it's right under our
nose Roger. Look out your side window
and you will see the motorway. I can
confirm the junction was dead ahead.
Luckily, one of us was awake.'

'Sorry Lewis, I've had a lot on my mind.'

'Well never mind that now, hold the
heading and be ready for your next
checkpoint, which is?'

'Err a small town with a railway line in six
minutes.'

'OK well don't miss it, and presumably
the next is the first of the disused airfields,
which is a turning point?'

'Yes, it is, four minutes later.'

'OK, well I'll stay awake until you reach
the disused airfield and turn on to your new
heading, then I'm going to sleep. If we don't
make it back to Linton, that's down to you,
Roger, so concentrate on what you are
doing.'

They reached the first disused airfield and
Roger turned on to his new heading. Soon,
snoring noises could be heard coming from
the right-hand seat. Roger decided he really

had to concentrate on what he was doing.

Half an hour later, Roger spotted Linton Airfield ahead. 'Linton Tower, Hotel-Tango returning from cross-country.'

'Roger Hotel-Tango. Join left-hand downwind for runway zero-eight, cleared to finals number one. QFE One-Zero-One-One.'

'Left hand downwind for zero-eight, number one, QFE One-Zero-One-One. Hotel-Tango.'

Roger set One-Zero-One-One on the subscale of the altimeter. *Hang on,* he thought, *I've not landed on zero-eight before. So I've got to approach from the other end. And left hand downwind?* Roger pictured it all in his mind and worked out where to aim for. He joined the circuit and descended on to finals.

'Hotel-Tango finals.'

'Hotel-Tango, cleared to land zero-eight.'

'Cleared land. Hotel-Tango.'

Roger landed on the numbers and taxied back to the club.

As he shut the aircraft down, he heard a yawn. 'Oh, are we home Roger? Excellent.'

Roger and Lewis left the aircraft and walked back to the club. 'Listen to me, Roger, you have the makings of an excellent pilot but you need to concentrate. Leave your problems at home. Now we need to think about getting your Nav and Met exams sorted out. You can't do your solo cross-country flight until you've passed them.'

They walked back into reception, and Lewis went straight into his office and shut the door.

'How did it go?' asked Mandy.

'Well I got back alright,' said Roger with a laugh, 'Are you going to join me in the bar when you finish?'

'You bet,' replied Mandy.

CHAPTER FORTY-FIVE

Roger walked into the bar. Fidel was behind the bar. 'Oh God, what's happened to your face, Roger?'

'Domestic bliss, Fidel. Hell knoweth no fury like a woman scorned.'

'They may need to rewrite that one in the future Roger. Gays can be even worse.'

'If you say so, Fidel. Pint please.'

Fidel started pouring him a pint. 'The green-eyed monster was it, Roger? Something to do with Mandy?'

'Yes, why do you ask?'

'Well, being behind the bar, you tend to pick up on all sorts of gossip. But I must say, at the moment, it's mostly about you and Mandy.'

'Oh well, as Oscar Wilde said, there is

only one thing in life worse than being talked about, and that is not being talked about.'

'Well, you must be doing pretty well then Roger,' said Fidel as he put the pint on the bar, 'Four pounds please.'

Roger put four pounds on the bar, turned and looked around the club.

Captain Flack and his crew were sitting together on a table. Sandy looked up and smiled at him, but her expression changed abruptly when she noticed his injuries. She got up and came over.

'Roger, what on earth has happened to your face?'

'It was a Greek night. I caught some plates with my face.'

'Oh, dear. Are you suing the restaurant?'

'Well it didn't happen in a restaurant, it was in my kitchen.'

Sandy looked puzzled. 'You had a Greek night in your kitchen?'

'More of a Greek breakfast really, and my wife was doing the throwing. Domestic bliss.'

'Oh, I see. Something to do with you and Mandy?'

'Yes. But I didn't realise everybody knew

about us.'

'Christ, this is a bloody flying club, Roger. Members can see things that are going to happen, long before they actually happen.'

'Well, we both went to Jersey together for the day, got fogged in and stayed the night. But it's far more complicated than that. Our spouses have got to like each other a bit too much as well.'

'OK, Roger. As you say it's very complicated, but if you ever need a shoulder to cry on, then let me know. I'll see you later.'

Sandy went back to her crew. As she sat down, Kyle got up and came over.

'Hello, Roger, been in the wars?'

'Yes, Kyle. Domestic bliss and all that.'

'Oh, dear. How about I cheer you up with one of my stories?'

'Please do. I do love your stories.'

'Well I've been thinking and I've got a couple for you today. A few years ago, when I worked for an Irish airline, I recognised Michael O'Leary travelling with us. Why he was travelling with us rather than his own airline, Ryanair, I don't know. Probably checking out the competition, I thought. When I came to serve him, he was looking at the menu. "Guinness only a pound a pint. That's cheaper than us. A pint of Guinness please." I'll get you I thought, so I said, "OK sir, now, would you like a glass with that?"'

Roger laughed. 'Poetic Justice! Now, what was the other story?'

'Well, I once had a passenger who was wearing the tightest pants I had ever seen on a man. So tight that they left absolutely nothing to the imagination. I couldn't work out how he had managed to put them on. Eventually, I just had to ask. So I went up to him and said, "how on earth do you get into those pants?" He looked me up and down, smiled, and said "Well you could start by buying me a drink."'

Roger laughed. 'You should write a book, Kyle. Confessions of an Air Steward.'

CHAPTER FORTY-SIX

George walked into the bar, clutching some paperwork.

Here comes George, thought Roger, *Oh, something is up, he's got a face as black as thunder.*

'Hello Roger, oh what on earth has happened to your face? Has Guy been giving you lessons on how to bump into radiators?'

'No, just domestic bliss. Don't ask.'

'Oh alright. Now, have you seen Steve about? I've got a bone to pick with him.'

'No, I've not seen him today. What's up?'

'You remember he got me the ladies watch from the bond? Well, it didn't work, so I took it back for a refund. The chap gave me thirty pounds back. I said I paid forty pounds. You didn't he said, and showed me the price list.'

'I thought Steve said they didn't do price lists.'

'Indeed he did. He's charged me ten pounds extra for the watch and I bet he's overcharged us all for the rest of the duty-free as well. That's why he told us they didn't do price lists. The bastard was making money out of all of us.'

'That's not very friendly.'

'Bloody right it's not. He's always trying to dodge his round, he's tighter than a camel's arse in a sandstorm. I shan't be flying with him any more. That's the end for me.'

'Are you sure, George? I thought you'd been flying with him for quite a few years.'

'I have, but there comes a point when all the bad things overwhelm the good. And the watch was the final straw.'

'You'll still be doing your trips though, won't you? I really enjoyed Le Touquet and Jernsey.'

'Oh yes. I'll probably find someone else to fly with. Having said that, what about you, Roger? You seem to have plenty of spare time and money.'

'Me? I haven't even got a bloody licence.'

'No, but you will have fairly soon. Lewis says you're doing really well. And think of the experience you'll gain sitting up the front in a pilot's seat. If the weather is good, you can even sit on the left-hand side. I'll help you all I can.'

'Well, sounds like an offer I can't refuse. I'd love to, George. Thanks.'

'I can show you how to use naviads like VORs and NDBs and that'll give you a head start for when you begin your IMC rating.'

'My IMC rating?'

'Yes, so you can fly in cloud on instruments, and navigate using radio beacons.'

'I'll look forward to that. Oh, you are in luck George, Steve's just walked in.'

George spun round. Steve spotted him and came over.

'Steve, your round I think,' said George, 'Two pints and whatever you want.'

'Oh, my round, is it? Are you sure?'

'Yes, I'm sure.'

Steve's face fell, but he turned and went to the bar.

'I thought you were having no more to do

with him,' said Roger.

'Well, I thought we might as well get one last pint off him,' said George, 'make up for the overcharging. He'll never admit what he's done, he'll make out it was all a dreadful mistake. I've known him for a long time.'

Steve returned from the bar, clutching three pints. 'Here you are boys, get your laughing gear around these.'

'Cheers,' said Roger.

'I hear you did your first cross-country today Roger,' said Steve, 'How did it go?'

'Well I'm back and I didn't get lost, so I think I did OK.'

'Good man,' said Steve. He turned to George. 'What's that print out under your arm, George?'

'Oh that,' said George, 'it's a price list from the bonded store.'

The colour drained from Steve's face, but he quickly recovered. 'Price list? Err, they told me they didn't do price lists.'

'Did they?' said George, 'they were quick enough to give me one when I took that faulty ladies watch back. They pointed out it only cost thirty pounds, not the forty pounds I paid you for it.'

'I'm sorry about that. I must have made a mistake when I was doing the working out.'

George held out his hand. 'So you owe me a tenner.'

'Err, yes. And you want it now?'

'Of course.'

Steve looked dismayed. He put his hand in his pocket and got out his wallet. He scrabbled about inside and found a ten-pound note. 'Here you are.'

'Thanks.'

'Right, well that's all sorted out. Now, what's our next flight going to be then, George? I thought perhaps La Rochelle, maybe for a weekend? Bob is always going on about it, La Rochelle this and La Rochelle that, waving his bloody hand with the pronunciation. What do you think?'

George looked Steve in the eye. 'Sorry Steve, I don't believe you made a mistake with the watch. I think you said there was no price list so you could overcharge us all for the duty-free and I'm fed up with you always trying to avoid your round. I've had enough, I don't want to fly with you any more.'

Steve looked stunned. He went white. He picked up his pint and downed the remaining beer, turned on his heel and left the club.

Roger looked at George. 'Bit harsh, I thought. He looked like you had hit him with a sledgehammer.'

'Well, it had to be said. No point in beating around the bush.'

CHAPTER FORTY-SEVEN

'Would you like another pint, Roger?' asked George.

'Yes please.'

George went to the bar. Kingsley came over. 'Yes George, what can I get you?'

'Two pints please.'

Kingsley started to pour. 'I've got my menu finished. I'll give you a copy and perhaps you'll let me know what you think?'

'Happy to.'

Kingsley put one pint on the bar, then reached underneath and produced a menu. 'There you are George. You can show it around, all feedback welcome.'

George started to look at the menu while Kingsley continued to pour the drinks.

'Two pints, George. Eight pounds please.'

181

George paid, and carried the drinks back to Roger.

'Thanks, George,' said Roger, 'what's on the piece of card?'

'It's Kingsley's new food menu. He wants some feedback.'

'Anything nice on there?'

'Well peppered steak, one of my favourites. Moules Frites, no doubt Bob will complain about the spelling or how it's done, a selection of home-made pies and things like burgers, chips etc. That's the evening menu. On the lunch menu there's lots of salads, quiches and other rubbish.'

'Yes, the evening menu sounds OK, but the lunch menu sounds more up Mandy's street than mine.'

'Is she joining you tonight?'

'Yes she is. Apparently, we are the talk of the bar, according to Fiddle and Sandy.'

'Well everyone likes a bit of gossip, and adultery is the preferred subject, I suppose.'

'I've never had an affair before, but I suppose it had to happen eventually. Alison and I had been having Olympic sex.'

'Olympic sex sounds good. If you've been having Olympic sex, why the affair?'

'Olympic sex George, once every four

years?'

'Oh, I see.'

'I think the problem was I never had sex with my wife before we married, George,' said Roger, 'Did you?'

'I'm not sure Roger, what was Alison's maiden name?'

'The only sex advice my Dad gave me was that you'll never understand a woman as long as you live. I think he was right.'

'I'm sure he was right, Roger. I gave up trying a long while ago, and moved on to something a little bit simpler, like quantum physics!'

'Did you ever read the book, Men are from Mars, Women are from Venus?'

'No, I wouldn't waste my time. I think a good woman should be like a good bar. Liquor in the front, poker in the rear.'

Roger laughed. 'Mandy is such an improvement on Alison. She enjoys life, she enjoys sex, and she's not always looking for something to moan about. She's —'

'She's what, Roger?'

Roger looked round. 'Hello Mandy, where did you spring from?'

'Oh, I was just standing here listening.'

'I was telling George how wonderful you

are. What would you like to drink?'

'G and T please.'

Roger went off to the bar.

'Have you seen the new food menu, Mandy?' asked George, passing the menu to her.

'No, I haven't, thanks George.'

Mandy read through the menu. 'Seems to be a fairly broad range of choices. I particularly like the lunchtime menu.'

'Eat a lot of rabbit food, do you?'

'Well, I do have to watch my figure.'

'Here's your G and T,' said Roger, 'Mandy, why don't you just eat what you like and let me watch your figure? I'd quite enjoy that.'

'Well there's certainly plenty to watch,' said Guy, joining the group.

'Oh hello, Guy. Trust you to arrive at the wrong moment,' said Mandy.

'I've never understood why women obsess over their figures,' said Guy.

'Well it's not only our figures Guy, we women like to look good all round,' said Mandy, 'As I've got older, I worry about all the wrinkles that have appeared on my face.'

'Easily cured,' said Guy, setting off to his stage. 'Take your bra off. That enormous

weight sinking will stretch all those wrinkles
out of your face in no time. You might
damage your kneecaps though!'

CHAPTER FORTY-EIGHT

Over on the stage, Guy commenced his disco.

'Good evening, Ladies and Gentlemen. Welcome to the Cloud Nine disco with your host, Prince Charles.'

'I'll start tonight as always by reading today's main stories from your local rag, the Linton, Fleawick and Moldon Evening Gazette.'

'My younger brother Edward has admitted in a rather frank interview that joining the Royal Marines was a mistake. He revealed he really wanted to be in the Hussars. Whose arse in particular though, he didn't specify.'

'Monica Lewinsky is in London this week celebrating a rather large birthday.

Amazing, isn't it. Doesn't seem five minutes ago she was going around the Oval Office on all fours.'

'And finally, Virgin Trains has come under a storm of criticism. Breakdowns, cancelled trains, points failures. Still, I think the name Virgin is quite apt, as you obviously can't go all the way on it!'

'So I'll start tonight's session with Last Train To Clarksville by The Monkees.'

The music started to play.

'Time to go,' said Mandy.

'I'll see you to your car,' said Roger.

'I thought you might.'

'Well, you did discover what the sharp object was last time. Maybe you could check it out again?'

'Maybe.'

They left the club and walked out into the car park. Mandy had parked in the far corner again.

Roger grabbed Mandy, pushed her up against the side of the car and kissed her.

'Oh,' said Mandy, 'that sharp object is still down there.'

She clicked her keyring and unlocked the car doors. 'Get in the back, so I can investigate properly.'

Roger opened the door and got in. Mandy followed. She unzipped his trousers and pulled them and his pants down.

'Now,' she said, 'let me have a good look.'

Suddenly, there was a bright flash.

'What the?' said Roger.

Another bright flash followed.

'Some pervert is taking pictures!' said Roger and quickly pulled his trousers up. 'I'll punch their lights out.'

He opened the door and there stood Alison and Dan, both holding a camera.

'Hello Roger and hello Mandy,' said Alison, 'sorry about the coitus interruptus, but we just dropped by to let you both know that we are starting divorce proceedings first thing tomorrow morning. Goodnight now.'

TO BE CONTINUED

If you have enjoyed reading this book, please leave a review on Amazon or where you purchased it.

Have you any stories from flying clubs or about flying that could feature in a forthcoming book?

Contact me: howard@lintonflying.club or visit www.lintonflying.club

Printed in Poland
by Amazon Fulfillment
Poland Sp. z o.o., Wrocław